Hey, TodaysGirls! Check out 2day's kewlest music, books, and stuff when u hit spiritgirl.com

Published in Nashville, Tennessee, by Tommy Nelson™, a division of Thomas Nelson, Inc.

Scripture quotations are from the *International Children's Bible®, New Century Version®:* Copyright © 1986, 1988, 1999 by Tommy Nelson™, a division of Thomas Nelson, Inc.

Creative director and series consultant: Dandi Daley Mackall
Computer programming consultant: Lucinda C. Thurman

Library of Congress Cataloging-in-Publication Data application has been made.

ISBN 0-8499-7583-2

Printed in the United States of America

00 01 02 03 04 05 PHX 0 9 8 7 6 5 4 3 2 1

CHAT FREAK

WRITTEN BY
Kristi Holl

CREATED BY
Terry K. Brown

Tommy
NELSON™
Thomas Nelson, Inc.
Nashville

Web Words

2 to/too

4 for

ACK! disgusted

AIMP always in my prayers

A/S/L age/sex/location

B4 before

BBL be back later

BBS be back soon

BD big deal

BF boyfriend

BFN bye for now

BRB be right back

BTW by the way

CU see you

Cuz because

CYAL8R see you later

Dunno don't know

Enuf enough

FWIW for what it's worth

FYI for your information

G2G or **GTG** I've got to go

GF girlfriend

GR8 great

H&K hug and kiss

IC I see

IN2 into

IRL in real life

JK just kidding

JLY Jesus loves you

JMO just my opinion

K okay

Kewl cool

KOTC kiss on the cheek

L8R later

LOL laugh out loud

LTNC long time no see

LY love you

NBD no big deal

NU new/knew

NW no way

OIC oh, I see

QT cutie

RO rock on

ROFL rolling on floor laughing

RU are you

SOL sooner or later

Splain explain

SWAK sealed with a kiss

SYS see you soon

Thanx (or) **thx** thanks

TNT till next time

TTFN ta ta for now

TTYL talk to you later

U you

U NO you know

UD you'd (you would)

UR your/you're/you are

WB welcome back

WBS write back soon

WTG way to go

Y why

(Note: Remember that capitalization may vary.)

iv

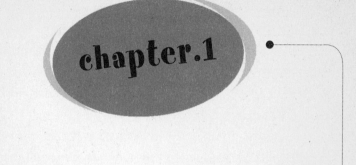

chapter.1

Just what I was looking for!" Morgan cried, digging behind the dried fruit to where she'd hidden her crispy M&M's. Clutching the bright blue bag, she smiled at her older sister. "I want these for the chat."

Morgan's sister, Maya, rolled her eyes, and then she reached into the fridge for a Diet Coke to have with her mini pretzels. "How do you ever expect to drop that baby fat eating like that?"

Morgan paused from pouring a handful of candy. "Do you really think I look fat?"

"I just think you'd want to look a bit more . . . sleek . . . for New York next week."

"Why? Who's going to be watching me?"

Maya looked her over from head to toe. "You're right. I'm the one looking at fashion design schools while you befriend old sea cows." She gave a delicate shudder. "Chow down."

"They're seals, not sea cows." Morgan glanced at the clock. "It's almost eight," she said, referring to their TodaysGirls.com scheduled chat with their friends. "Can I use your computer for a change? You can use my laptop."

"Not a chance." Maya sipped her soda as she left the room.

Sighing, Morgan unplugged the family's phone and snapped the line into her laptop. She was sick of Maya always getting her way. That teen line belonged to her too, but Maya hogged it. That left Morgan on the family line, which limited her to only a half-hour chat. She wanted more time than that.

In less than a minute, she was logged on. The purple icon— Welcome to TodaysGirls.com—with its magenta background lit up her screen. Amber's Thought for the Day popped open at the top.

Keep your eyes focused on what is right. Keep looking straight ahead to what is good. Proverbs 4:25
      Let's focus on the real meaning of Easter this week-- and it's not chocolate!

Morgan smiled as she clicked into the chat room. Bren and Jamie were already deciding whether one-piece swimming suits looked better on Bren, or whether she looked more stunning when clad in two pieces. *One swimsuit for me is enough,* Morgan thought. But Maya jumped right in, giving her professional advice.

"OK, let's try a new topic," Morgan said aloud, hesitating a moment before popping a handful of M&M's into her mouth. The sooner they talked about their spring break plans, the sooner they'd end their chat session—and then she could surf the Web on her own.

jellybean: can U believe spring break is almost here? I'm
    so excited!
nycbutterfly: it's about time U wrote something. I thought
    you'd died. Or R U pouting cuz you're in the kitchen?
chicChick: bet it's easy 2 hook into different lines when
    U have UR own laptop! I wish I had one. then I could
    shop whenever I wanted!

Hooking up the laptop was a cinch, actually. The lack of time online was the problem. Morgan had people on the Web to talk to . . . and places to be. *Let's keep this moving,* she thought.

jellybean: What about those French boys, Bren?
chicChick: Mais oui! April in Paris. I'm so psyched!
TX2step: Lucky! You get to leave early and miss more
    school. I don't head to TX till the weekend.
faithful1: I need 2 stay home and make $$. Gotta save!

TX2step: We're gonna spend the week on Padre Island. It'll be a whole nother thing swimming w/o a timer!

rembrandt: UR making me jealous! My vacation will B working all week w/Amber @ the Gnosh while the owner's daughters go out on the town!

nycbutterfly: I only wish! Visiting colleges will be fun, but nothing's like shoppin downtown NYC.

jellybean: All right, that covers "Todaysgirls Do Spring Break." Texas. Paris. NYC. Indiana. We're still going 2 try 2 meet online @ eight every night, right?

nycbutterfly: What's your hurry, Morg? It's only 8:25. I think U can afford 5 more minutes.

faithful1: Wait! I don't even know what UR doin' in NYC!

jellybean: Hangin @ the Aquarium 4 Wildlife Conservation on Coney Island--it's 4 my Save the Seals project. I'm volunteering 2 afternoons while mom & dad take Maya 2 do her school thing. Then I want 2 start a Save the Seals group here.

nycbutterfly: Because there R so many seals in Indiana to B saved. :-)

rembrandt: sounds too educational! 2 much 4 me on spring break.

nycbutterfly: I'm much more excited about seeing the city again. Lights, crowds, taxis, skyscrapers, Fifth Ave! I hope I find the perfect college. It'd be so cool to go to college in NYC!!

Morgan tapped her foot as the chat scrolled down the screen. This was taking forever. At this rate she'd never even get to check her e-mail. Hmm, maybe she could click over and do that now.

jellybean: BRB

She exited TodaysGirls.com and clicked to her personal e-mail account. She'd made friends around the world at the GlobalBuddies.com site, and sure enough, there were three letters from overseas. The one from the UK was first. She read it eagerly. Then, scanning more quickly, she moved to the second one, then the third . . .

"Morgan!" Mrs. Cross called from the living room. "It's 8:30. Hint, hint."

"OK." Morgan reentered their private chat room long enough to say good-bye.

TX2step: hey, where'd U go?
jellybean: Sorry. Time 2 sign off. C U all tomorrow.

Morgan logged off and plugged the cord back into her parents' white phone. As she replaced her M&M's in their hiding place, the phone rang. Morgan picked up the family line, but heard nothing but a dial tone. It was their see-through blue teen phone ringing instead. And that meant one thing: Maya had logged off of their Web site!

"Hello," Morgan said into the receiver.

"Hey. This is Darryl. Is Maya home?"

"Oh. Hi, Darryl. Hold on a minute."

Morgan could hear Maya talking to their mother in the living room, and she started to get her. Then she stopped. Was she crazy? She'd never get to talk to her GlobalBuddies if Maya gabbed with Darryl. Maya always used their teen line. It was Morgan's turn. And Darryl would surely call again. Or Maya could call him. Retracing her steps to the phone, Morgan picked up the receiver. "Um, Darryl . . . Maya can't come to the phone now. I'll have her call you back."

After I have some time online first, she added to herself as she hung up. It was only fair, after all. She was supposed to share that line with Maya and their older brother. Jacob rarely used it, Morgan had to fight for it, and Maya acted like she owned it and everyone should get special permission from her to use it. It was time for Morgan to have a turn.

A minute later Maya strolled into the kitchen. "Stay off our phone line," she ordered, poking her head into the refrigerator. She emerged with another Diet Coke. "I'm going to watch a movie, and somebody might call, so don't tie it up."

"I'm just going to my room to do homework," Morgan said, packing up her laptop. She waited on the stairs until she heard the opening strains of Maya's favorite movie coming from the den, then she hurried upstairs. She passed her own room and continued down the hall to Maya's room, where the other teen line was located. Within seconds, she was in the GlobalBuddies chat room. Half an hour later, Maya yelled up the stairs, "You'd better not be tying up the phone line, Morgan!"

Morgan jumped, jerked out of her imaginary world. "I'm not!" she yelled back, holding her breath. *I'll get off in just a minute,* she promised herself, but she lost track of time again as she got involved trying to help a girl having trouble with her boyfriend. Morgan liked that people could talk to her about anything. They knew she was a good listener. Glancing at the clock some time later, she realized Maya's movie had to be almost over. "Back L8R," she wrote and hit the *Exit* button.

After shutting down, Morgan took her laptop to her room and climbed into her pajamas. When Maya stopped in her doorway a few minutes later, Morgan was sprawled across her bed among Save the Seals brochures and pamphlets. "Been working hard?" her sister asked.

"Yup," Morgan lied, the guilt nearly choking her. "Good movie?"

"You know how *Ever After* ends: together at last." She clutched her heart with a sigh. Then Maya frowned and pulled on her bottom lip. "Why doesn't my life go like that? That jerk Darryl didn't call, did he? Oh, never mind. Who cares?" Without waiting for an answer, she cruised down the hall toward her bedroom.

Morgan waited till her parents came and said "good night," then she gathered and stacked up her brochures. Finally, the house was quiet. Even her big brother had crashed early. Listening in the hall, Morgan heard nothing. Grabbing her laptop, she snuck back down to the kitchen, where she could reconnect. The green screen made an eerie glow in the kitchen as she joined GlobalBuddies.com. So cool to be able to find friends any time of the day or night. Two hours later her "battery low" sign blinked, and regretfully she logged off. Stumbling upstairs, she groaned inwardly at how soon her alarm would go off.

At swim practice before school Wednesday morning, Morgan yawned while treading water and gulped chlorinated pool water. She coughed until her eyes ran. She wished she could convince their coach, Harrison Short, to let her skip her warmup laps that morning. She needed to save her strength for the big meet right after school that day. Morning light filtered though the dusty windows and reflected off Coach's glasses, so she couldn't tell if he was watching her or not.

Still yawning, Morgan floated on her back over to the fourth lane, right next to Alex. If only she could close her bleary eyes and sink into a deep sleep right there. Morgan saw Alex moving slowly away through the water in a sidestroke. Morgan floated till Alex swam back, reading the large record board that stated all the swim records.

Alex treaded water beside her and asked, "So whadya do last night?"

"I met some of the coolest people online—they're from all

over the world. I mean like Scotland and Zambia and places like that. There was a girl who lives on a farm in Wales and a boy who's learning to drive in Germany. You wouldn't even believe the variety of people at GlobalBuddies."

Alex raised an eyebrow as Morgan yawned again. "What is wrong with you? Did you talk all night?"

"Well, not quite," Morgan said sheepishly. "Time just passes so fast in the chat rooms."

"OK team," Coach shouted. "Time for a couple 500-yard warmups. Make 'em easy ones because of tonight's big meet. Then we'll do one relay where I time you."

They pushed off down the length of the 25-yard pool to do the laps, trying to stay out of each other's way. For meets, red-and-white lane markers would separate them.

After their laps, they lined up for the relay. Amber, Morgan, Maya, and Alex always did the backstroke, breaststroke, butterfly, and freestyle, in that order. Before meets, electronic touch pads were lowered against the side of the shallow end of the pool to provide accurate swim times. But for now, Coach just set his stopwatch and blew his whistle.

When Morgan followed Amber, her arms and legs felt so heavy and slow that she might as well have been swimming through pudding. When she dragged herself out of the pool, she could tell by the look on Coach's face that her time was way off.

"Just what have you been up to, young lady?"

"Wha—What do you mean?"

"Are you sick?"

Morgan stared at the blue-and-white tile deck. "No, just a little tired."

"Well, let's hope you pick up speed by this afternoon," he snapped. "It won't matter if your teammates sail along if you're chugging behind like a tugboat." He turned to time Maya, then Alex.

Morgan's eyes welled up with tears at his sharp tone, and she dived back in the pool to swim more laps. She should have known better than to get back online after everyone went to bed. She always ended up staying and chatting longer than she had intended.

Ten minutes later, Morgan walked past the door to Coach's office and the small storage area, following her friends into the girls' locker room. Embarrassed by her time, she kept her eyes carefully fixed on the trail of wet footprints. At the far end of the dressing room, Maya slammed her locker shut while she fumed to Amber. "He as good as stood me up last night. Phone calls count. When guys say they'll call and don't, it's an official stand up."

"You got stood up? By who?" Alex asked.

Amber grabbed her towel. "By Darryl. If you can count the phone," explained Amber. "I'm sure he tried, Maya. Maybe he got sick or something."

"Fat chance," Maya snapped. "When they say 'I'll call,' and they don't, it counts. At least I count it. And I won't forget it."

Something in Morgan's stomach twisted. She'd had no idea that Maya was actually expecting Darryl's call.

"Why make such a big deal about it, Maya?" Alex asked. "You have a hundred guys hangin' on you all the time. It's just one stupid phone call."

"Hey, it's Darryl's loss," Maya snarled, flouncing off to the showers, but not before Morgan glimpsed her hurt expression.

Morgan and Alex scooted into their first block biology class twenty minutes later with just seconds to spare.

"Hello, ladies," Jared called from across the room. "Ready to save the world?" He gestured toward the books, tagboard, and newspapers spread out on the back table for their project.

Morgan shrugged at her stocky friend. "Well, we'll save the seals, anyway."

Alex plopped down at her own desk, baggy jeans dragging, and pulled her wet curly hair back into a ponytail. "You guys are lucky. Our group got the platypus. Talk about *ugly*. You'd think people would wanna get rid of the homely critters."

"Where's Ty?" Morgan asked, referring to the third member of their group. Just then the tardy buzzer sounded.

"In the library getting some nature magazine. Ms. Duchovny said it had a good seal article."

Ms. Duchovny waited for quiet, then rattled off the attendance list. She still didn't know their names, although she'd subbed for Mr. Kistler for a whole week already while he was having knee surgery. As she read, Morgan leaned on one elbow and scrunched her hair, still wet from practice. She'd stayed in the shower longer than necessary, avoiding Maya.

Morgan sank deeper in guilt as she remembered the hurt look on Maya's face about the missed phone call. Still, the teen line wasn't just for Maya's social life. How else could she get any decent time on the Net? And it wasn't like she wasted her time there. She was friendly and tried to help people, didn't she?

Ms. Duchovny's voice permeated Morgan's thoughts, and she glanced up. An aqua ribbon surrounded Ms. D.'s thin brown ponytail, and a peach plastic earring dangled on each side of her triangular face. A turtleneck topped the pale, faded jeans. "If you have any questions about your group projects, get them answered before Friday. I'll be out of town all next week for spring break, and your projects are due when we come back the day after Easter." She tossed her head, making her earrings and ponytail jerk. "Let's get to work."

Just then Tyler shuffled into the room, clutching the nature magazine he'd rolled into a tube. "Here." It unfolded on the table, the cover showing several seals tangled in fishing nets. "We can use this." He flipped it open to the main article.

"Seal Conservation Society Fights Marine Rescue Unit." Morgan frowned at the title. "I'll try to find out more about this when I'm in New York, and I'll e-mail it back to you guys." She yawned so wide her jaws popped, and she pressed on her throbbing forehead. "Um, you work on the reports and charts while

I'm gone, and I'll write up stuff after volunteering there and see about starting a Save the Seals group here at school."

Jared rolled his eyes and saluted. "Yes, sir! Morgan, sir!"

Ty rubbed a hand over his pockmarked cheek. "Should we meet before you leave town to divide up the work?" he asked quietly. "Like maybe Friday night?"

"Do homework on Friday night? Are you crazy?"

Ty glanced away. "OK, Thursday night."

Jared shrugged his broad shoulders. "Big track meet out of town. I won't be back till late." Jared already held a record in the shot put. "How about tonight?"

"Can't." Morgan rubbed the back of her neck. "Blairsburg swim meet."

Ty rolled back and forth on the balls of his feet, the extra-long tail of his plaid shirt moving with him. "Like I said in the first place, what about Friday night?"

"No choice, I guess." Morgan stacked their resource books. "What time?"

"Seven o'clock work for you both?" Jared asked. At their nods, he said, "OK, community college library at seven. We can probably use a conference room."

When the bell rang an hour later, Ty, Jared, and Morgan were still talking as they joined the crowd streaming out the door. However, Morgan stopped in mid-sentence at the sound of a familiar voice near the water fountain.

Maya's clipped words carried over the noise in the hall. "I said don't talk to me, Darryl Hume. If it wasn't important enough for you to call last night, don't bother talking to me now!" Maya pivoted on her heel and stomped in the direction of the cafeteria.

"But I did call!" Darryl shouted after her.

Morgan's throat tightened as she stepped behind Jared before Darryl could see her.

"Wow." Jared crossed his arms across his barrel-shaped chest and looked at Darryl's departing back. "Now you don't see that every day. One of the popular guys getting leveled down."

"Publicly," added Morgan. "By my sister."

She wanted to crawl into a hole and disappear. She'd caused the whole problem between Maya and Darryl. And if the tightness in her throat and stomach meant anything, she was about to be found out for sure.

chapter.2

Morgan knew from the minute she slipped into the water at the swim meet after school that a disaster was on the horizon—and she was powerless to stop its advance.

Her warmup laps alongside Alex felt slow and heavy, and her arms were leaden as they stretched and reached and pulled back in her breaststroke. What was she thinking, staying online till all hours? Seeing Jared in the stands—with his grin and "thumbs-up" sign—did nothing to lift the black cloud she felt sure followed her up and down lane four.

Dragging herself out of the pool, Morgan glanced toward Coach, but he was busy giving Maya some pep talk. Before Morgan had time to worry anymore, the first race was announced. By the end of the fourth race, it was apparent that it would be a neck and neck combat between Edgewood and

Blairsburg. Pressure built inside Morgan, while at the same time she felt far removed from the meet. It was as if the yelling and cheering were going on around her, but she saw it through a glass bubble and heard it from under water.

"Hey!"

Morgan jerked as Coach snapped his fingers in front of her nose.

"Earth to Morgan. Earth to Morgan." His wink softened the wake-up call, and he gazed at her quizzically. "You OK?"

Morgan forced a smile. "You bet! After my 500, I'll really pour it on for the relay."

"That's what I wanted to talk to you about." Coach twisted his whistle chain. "I'm pulling you from the 500 to save your strength for the end."

"What!"

He draped his arm over her shoulders. "I hope you're not coming down with something, but your time was off this morning, and I could see in the warmups that you're still struggling. Is your neck hurting? You're holding it funny."

"Um, some. Not bad," she lied, fingering the knot at the base of her skull.

"Well, the team needs all your energy for the relay."

"But won't we need my points from the 500?"

"I'll have Brianna take your place just this once. Hopefully she'll pull a few points down for us. It's the relay that really counts today. OK?"

Morgan took a deep breath and stared at her brightly painted toenails. "Sure," she replied, a little hurt. "It's OK."

The rest of the meet passed in a blur for Morgan. She sat on the bench, doing her best to cheer Brianna in the race she herself should have won. As the afternoon wore on, the tension in the stands grew, the cheering echoing in Morgan's head. Usually she loved the frenzy of the crowd, but today it made her head hurt worse. She watched the scoreboard as the first- through sixth-place swimmers' times were posted. Sometimes Edgewood inched ahead, sometimes Blairsburg.

Finally their relay was called. After tucking her hair up under her cap, Morgan joined her relay team behind the starting blocks in the shallow end of the pool. Amber shot forward first, her backstroke powerful, and she finished a full stroke ahead of the next-fastest team. It gave them a good solid lead, but did little to ease Morgan's anxiety. She followed Amber, and if she could only keep the lead, she'd be happy.

But lack of sleep and the neck cramp from hunching over the computer half the night prevented that. Morgan had a sick feeling the moment she pushed off in her breaststroke. It was like swimming through liquid quicksand. Although her lungs felt ready to burst from the exertion, the girl from Blairsburg in lane three slowly pulled even with her. Then, no matter how Morgan strained, she fell behind, stroke by agonizing stroke. By the time she'd flipped around and started churning back down lane four, she was nearly a full stroke behind. She never caught up.

Blairsburg fans erupted into screams, but Morgan didn't even look at the clock. She knew without asking that it was her worst time ever. Unless Alex and her sister could make up the lost time, they'd lose the race—and the meet. Head hanging, she stood behind Amber, who screamed for Maya, then Alex. Morgan joined in, praying that they'd win. Maya regained half the ground Morgan had lost, and Alex most of the rest. She was less than a foot behind the Blairsburg girl when they touched the electronic pads.

Morgan glanced up. According to the final score, they'd lost the meet by five measly points.

By the time she congratulated the winners, picked up their wet towels, and ventured a peek at the bench, all Morgan saw were the backs of her teammates as they trudged off to the locker room. She paused, then followed, pushing the door open and padding down the rows of lockers to where the Edgewood team was dressing.

"Well, did you fall asleep out there, Morgan?" Maya snapped.

"Maya, don't," Amber cautioned. "She didn't do it on purpose."

"I don't care! Do you know how big this meet was for us to win? She let us down, and it could have been prevented."

"You don't know that!" Amber said.

Alex frowned. "Did you get *any* sleep last night?"

"Huh!" Maya swung around. "No! She was up half the night

18

again with her chat room friends while her *real* friends and family were counting on her."

"Is that true?" Amber asked. "Say, is that why you have neck cramps?"

"Yes, it's true," Maya snapped. "Maybe we'd get farther with her if we called ourselves the Edgewood Cyber Swimmers."

Morgan grabbed her towel and gym bag and headed toward the showers. Not until she had the water running hot and steamy over her did she allow the tears to come.

Morgan fled to her room when she got home. She intended to avoid Maya at all costs. It was lonely, but loneliness was better than her sarcasm. When she heard her parents come home from work, Morgan hurried down, anxious for some sympathy. However, she overheard something that made her freeze.

A kitchen cupboard door slammed, then a pan was banged down on the stove. "I understand what you're saying, honey," her mom said, "but could you really run two restaurants? Seems you have your hands full with the Gnosh Pit alone."

"Well, what if I hired another manager? It's the perfect time to do this, what with being in New York next week for the management seminar. We could fly back and forth and keep an eye on both places." He paused. "Now be honest, don't you miss the city?"

"Well sure, especially the outlets for my art." Her mom laughed. "Even with the college, Edgewood is a bit short in the gallery department."

"With Maya wanting to go to college in New York eventually, it's a perfect solution."

Barely breathing, Morgan backed slowly up the stairs. She couldn't believe it! Her parents were talking about opening another restaurant and *moving* to New York! Next week's spring break vacation was no simple trip to the city for her dad's restaurant management seminar or her mom's meeting with a gallery owner. Morgan's eyes opened wide. She bet her mom wanted to talk to that gallery owner about a job there! All because Maya wanted a New York college, they were ready to uproot the whole family without even asking her! Didn't her feelings count for anything? Why was it always Maya that mattered?

Morgan was so silent during supper that even her brother, Jacob, noticed. "What's up, squirt?" he asked, tugging on her hair.

"Oh, nothin'."

Maya waved her forkful of salad in Morgan's direction. "She's bummed out after losing the whole swim meet for us today!"

"Maya, stop it this minute." Their dad's voice was sharp. "Everyone has an off day, even you. So that's enough, understand?"

Maya nodded, but shot a look full of daggers at Morgan. Actually Morgan didn't mind. She was glad her parents thought her silence was due to losing the meet. She couldn't bring herself to confront them about the *real* reason for the New York trip.

After picking at her pasta salad for fifteen minutes, she asked to be excused and hurried upstairs. She needed a friend, and she needed one badly. No one on the swim team was happy with her, that was for sure. But luckily she had GlobalBuddies.com.

Upstairs in Maya's room, she plugged in her laptop and logged on using their teen line. In no time at all, she was in the room. She read their ad as the chatware loaded: "GlobalBuddies is the best online friendship network on the Internet and gets more than 3 million hits every month. You can use Global-Buddies Chat to talk online with GlobalBuddies all over the world. Click here for options."

She clicked on the Listing by Age & Gender section, then proceeded to the teen girls' bulletin board. Morgan leaned close to the screen. What new questions had been posted since last night? She much preferred talking about someone else's problems. That way she didn't have to think about her own.

A message from ANNA caught her eye, maybe because it was a parent problem:

Can anyone out there help me? I'm getting really torked at my mom. Every meal she watches me and comments on my weight. Like tonight she asked me three times was I sure I wasn't losing weight? I swear she counted every bite I took! She's just jealous that she's fat and I'm not. I try to watch what I eat, but I do NOT have an eating disorder like she thinks. What can I do? HELLLLLLPPPP!!!!

Now this is something I know about, Morgan thought. She'd heard the same conversation a million times between her mom and Maya. Morgan wrote back:

Dear ANNA: Don't worry. Your problem with your mom sounds perfectly normal. My mom constantly says the same thing to my older sister, but my sister doesn't have an eating disorder either. Moms just worry. Most people watch what they eat. Just rest assured that you're perfectly normal. Try to ignore your mom. She's probably just heard too much in the news about anorexia and then overreacts. BTW, if you want to private e-mail, send it to jellybean14@hotmail.com. Good luck!

Hopefully she'll e-mail me, Morgan thought. *It'd be nice if* someone *appreciated me.*

"Hey, get off that phone," Maya snapped.

Morgan jumped. "You scared me! Don't sneak up on me like that."

"Sneak up on you? This is *my* room, remember?" Maya reached over with the mouse and closed the window.

"Hey, I wasn't done!"

"You are now. It's eight o'clock and I'm getting online with *real* people. Are you joining us from the kitchen?"

Morgan unplugged her laptop and picked it up. The last thing she needed was to go into TodaysGirls.com and hear a rehashing of the lost swim meet. "Nope. I'm going to bed. I have a ripping headache anyway."

"Get a clue *why*, Morgan."

Morgan left the room and trudged down the hall. She was in bed with the covers up to her eyes within five minutes. She just wanted this awful day to be over.

Between classes on Thursday, Morgan spent her time dodging Darryl. After seeing him in the halls twice, in the cafeteria, and in the library, she realized he was dogging her steps. She knew why. Maya was avoiding him at school and wouldn't take his calls at home.

Morgan knew he had every right to confront her and make her tell Maya the truth. But she couldn't handle it yet. One more attack from her big sister this week would be one too many.

chapter.3

On Friday morning, Ms. Duchovny told them all to report to the library to work on their projects. "I'm leaving for New York tomorrow," Morgan explained to her teacher. "We're doing the project online together next week, so can we work in the computer lab? I want to show Jared and Ty some sites I found."

The teacher agreed, so during first period, Morgan perched in front of a computer while Ty and Jared leaned over her shoulder. "You have to see this cool site I found yesterday." She logged on, typed in her password, and waited to connect. Then she typed in http://www.tmmc.org. "This is the Marine Mammal Center. Besides all these articles on seals, look at this." She scrolled down to the bottom of the page where a blinking sign begged them to Adopt-A-Seal!

Jared read over her shoulder. "'For only $30 you can adopt one of our special patients. Each adoptee is a successfully rehabilitated patient released back into the wild. For your $30 gift, you will receive a beautiful 5x7 portrait of your adoptee, complete with personalized Certificate of Adoption, animal biography, and a recent issue of our newsletter.'"

Morgan grinned. "I thought at the end of our report I'd ask the class to donate to this, and our class could adopt a seal. What do you think?"

"Great idea," Jared said.

"Half a great idea anyway," Ty agreed.

Morgan frowned. "What do you mean?"

"Well, how about if we three chip in and adopt a seal ourselves? Then for the report we could show our portrait and adoption certificate, then ask the class to donate toward this other stuff." He pointed a dirty fingernail at the screen, where it said that donated money would provide food for malnourished seals, antibiotics for injuries, and x-rays for fractured flippers and surgery.

Jared nodded. "I agree with Ty. If we have that portrait and adoption certificate, and show that we laid down our own money, it will have more impact. They'd be more likely to chip in then." He pulled his wallet from his back pocket. "I've got ten bucks I can donate." He gave it to Morgan.

Morgan unzipped her tiny shoulder purse. "I can donate ten dollars, too. What about you, Ty?"

Tyler stuck his hands in his pockets, then shrugged. "I left my money at home, but I'll bring my part tonight."

"OK, then I'll mail it in tomorrow before the post office closes." Morgan took the twenty dollars and stuck it inside her geometry book. "This will be more persuasive."

"Was that all?" Ty asked.

"No. While we're here, I want to show you my favorite site." Morgan typed in GlobalBuddies.com and waited for the site to load. "We have to make it clear that seals are in danger everywhere in the world."

"I've got statistics on that already," Ty said.

"Yes, but I thought personal stories would make the statistics real." Morgan glanced over her shoulder at him. "Personal stories will make kids want to donate money."

"So what's GlobalBuddies got to do with anything?" Jared asked.

"Here. Look." Morgan read aloud. "'GlobalBuddies is the electronic version of the traditional penpal service. Introduce yourself and make friends worldwide. Then enter Global-Buddies Chat to talk online with GlobalBuddies all over the world.'"

Jared whistled. "Three million hits per month? That's a lot of hits. And they're from all over."

"My point exactly." Morgan clicked over to the Listing by Hobby and Interest section. "You can find interests here that match your own and talk to people, and you can post questions for their bulletin board." She clicked over to *Post-A-Note!* to show them.

"So what?" Ty asked. "I don't get it."

"I'll post a note in the science section and ask if anyone lives near a place where seals are endangered. I'll ask for personal stories." Morgan typed her question. "Then we'll use them for our reports."

"Your online name is Jellybean?" Jared snorted. "Isn't that what your dad calls you?"

Morgan elbowed him in the ribs without glancing up. "Next week I'll take my laptop to New York with me, so I'll collect whatever stories get posted and e-mail them to you guys. You can decide where in your reports to use them. I'll be visiting the Aquarium for Wildlife Conservation to interview the people who take care of the seals there." She closed out the window then sighed and sat back. "Well, am I brilliant or what? Applaud if you like. Or throw money."

The bell rang then, and Morgan grabbed her books to head out the door behind the boys.

"Remember the library tonight," Jared said. "Bring all your info uptown and we'll finalize stuff before you go tomorrow. Then we'll know what we're each responsible for."

"I'll be there," Morgan promised.

Just before she rounded the corner by the music room, she heard a voice call out her name. She froze. *Darryl!*

Without a backward glance, Morgan ducked into the girls'

rest room and hid in a stall until she was sure Darryl would have had to leave. Peering around the corner, she checked both directions before scooting into Mr. Myers's vocal music room as the last buzzer sounded.

Morgan hurried home after school to log some time online with her GlobalBuddies before supper.

"Hey, Morg," called Jacob. "How's it goin'?"

"Hey yourself. Did you eat all of those?" Morgan pointed to Jacob's almost empty bowl of Fritos.

"Nope. The bag's on the shelf. I have to save room for all the travel junk food. And we're stopping somewhere on our way out of town."

"Lucky! Who knows what *we're* eating tonight!" Morgan said, swatting him on the shoulder. "So, are you heading out soon?"

"In just a few. I packed already. Pete and the guys will be here to pick me up any minute."

"You're going to have a blast."

Morgan took her own bowl of Fritos with her to Maya's room, where she logged online using their teen line. Lucky for her that Maya was doing last-minute shopping, so Morgan could chat undisturbed. Crunching the greasy chips, she entered GlobalBuddies.com and clicked on *Post-A-Note!* She knew it was way early for any replies, but there was a chance. When she clicked on her request, she was surprised to find three responses already.

One was from Mick in Australia:

Our Marine Rescue Unit cares for sick and injured marine mammals. We see New Zealand fur seals and Sub Antarctic fur seals here.

Mary in Canada wrote:

Here in British Columbia we have a wildlife rehab facility. We specialize in alternative medicine like herbal treatments and physical therapy. Last year we treated 42 harbour seals and one Northern fur seal. We have an 80% survival rate at this time.

And Jeff from Hawaii wrote:

We try to protect our endangered Hawaiian monk seals here. Several have been born on Maui in the last few years. Even though we have the Marine Mammal Protection Act and the Endangered Species Act. we still have to use yellow police tape to keep people on the beaches away from a hauled out seal.

Morgan scribbled the information in her notebook, quickly thanked each person for their information, then clicked over to the GlobalBuddies Chat room. Maybe the people who'd responded to her question were still there.

jellybean14: anyone here that answered my question about
   seals?

last__wish: what question about seals?

janine: what kind of seals?

jellybean14: the flipper kind. I'm doing this big report on
   endangered seals and wanted 2 talk 2 anyone with experience with them.

last__wish: I don't have experience, but I live near the Marine
   Mammal Center in Santa Barbara.

janine: is that California?

last__wish: yup. they rescue seals there, like harbour seals &
   Northern elephant seals & some fur seals.

jellybean14: have U been there?

last__wish: once. but after I saw a baby seal tangled up & cut
   by fish line, i never went back

jellybean14: isn't that sad?! that's just the kind of thing i want
   2 help prevent!

last__wish: if U R in CA, you could visit there.

jellybean14: wish i could, but i'm in indiana.

They continued to chat about school and the stuff last_wish
loved about California—movie screenings, surfers, whale-
watching—which all sounded a lot more exciting than anything
Morgan did in Edgewood.

last__wish: i gotta go. meds r making me sleepy.

jellybean14: meds?

last__wish: medication.

jellybean14: 4 what?

last__wish: pain medication 4 my cancer.

Morgan gasped when she read his reply. A kid with cancer? How scary!

jellybean14: i'm really sorry. does UR cancer have something
    2 do with UR screen name?

last__wish: ya, my last wish is 2 see my mom taken care of
    B4 I die. she's all alone. GTG rest. good luck with UR seals.

jellybean14: thanks. hope I run into U again soon. C U

Morgan sat motionless for a moment, stunned by last_wish's words. How would it feel to know you were dying from cancer at such a young age? She could barely imagine it. Absent-mindedly, she clicked on her personal e-mail icon and watched the new messages load. She spotted one right away from ANNA:

Dear jellybean, thanks for the advice about my mom. It worked. I decided to just listen to her, but not get excited about it. You're right that she's probably just overreacting from everything that's in the news about eating disorders. If I keep quiet, she'll see that I'm fine and hopefully stop nagging me. Thanks for listening! ANNA

Morgan smiled as she hit the *Reply* button. It felt good to have someone *thank* her for her support.

Dear ANNA: I'm glad I could help you! You're doing the right thing just to listen to your mom's lectures but not react. Don't let her fear rule your life. She needs to get a grip and trust you more. Aren't parents hard to handle sometimes? Keep me posted.

"Hey, you're the chat queen these days, smorgeous." Morgan jumped at Jacob's voice right behind her. "I mean . . . you hardly watch TV anymore."

"So what?" Morgan mumbled.

"MORGAN."

"What?" Annoyed, she looked over her shoulder at Jacob, who was cracking his knuckles.

"I'm heading out now. Pete's here. So, I'll see you. Have fun in New York, all right?"

"Yeah, you too. Just bring me back something!" She jumped up and gave her big brother a hug, then watched him sling his bag over his shoulder and clomp down the stairs to his waiting friend below.

Morgan followed more slowly, heading to the kitchen to refill her Fritos bowl. Just then she heard the chug-chug of Maya's ancient Volkswagen Beetle, Mr. Beep, in the driveway.

"Morgan Cross!" Maya's shout was accompanied by the

sound of the front door slamming. "Morgan! Did you talk to Darryl Tuesday night?" Maya's words grew louder as she stormed through the hallway. "Did you tell him that I couldn't come to the phone?"

"Um, Tuesday? I can't remember. I might have said something like that." Morgan glanced at her sister's furious scowl. "OK. That's what I said."

"I can't believe you. That is so lame, Morgan. It's beyond lame. You knew he called. I asked you and asked you while I was watching that movie if you were tying up the line, and you said no. Thanks to you, I called Darryl a liar. In front of the football team. And most of the swim team." Maya marched over to where Morgan was pouring chips. "I have never, *ever* kept you from an important call."

"It was just Darryl. I thought he would call ba—"

"Just Darryl? I tell you when Jared calls. Like he's even worth worrying about." Maya stuck her finger in Morgan's face. "Just because real guys don't call you is no reason for you to trash my social life."

"Maya, I'm not trying to trash your social life. But you do get to use the phone line a lot more than I do. I just wanted some time—"

"You think those online weirdos are friends, but they're not. They're strangers. They don't even know you. In fact, *I* should be so lucky!" Maya stormed out of the kitchen, and seconds later the TV in the den blared with a talk show.

Morgan's mouth was suddenly dry, and she decided to take a

glass of juice back to the computer. As she stood in front of the ice dispenser to fill her glass, she studied an old snapshot stuck there with a magnet. She and Maya had been three and five at the time. The picture had been taken after Morgan gave herself a white beard with Dad's shaving cream. Maya was wiping it off with the hem of her dress. Looking at the two round faces made Morgan's eyes sting. Maya was such a pain sometimes, but she was still her big sis.

"Morgan," her dad said from behind her chair. She'd barely noticed his shadow looming over her. "It's time for dinner."

"I'm not too hungry, Dad."

"It's no wonder with supplies like this." Dad nudged the nearly empty Fritos bowl.

"Jacob had some, too."

"I'm sure he did. Did he get off all right?"

"I think so."

"Morgan, switch that thing off." He tugged on her arm. "Your mother made some vegetarian dish that I'm sure she and Maya will love. Time to go act like we love it, too."

"But I'm talking with a girl from the UK."

Dad tapped his index finger on the glass above the "close screen" box. "Click that. Or I will. It's dinnertime."

During dinner, Morgan dished up the smallest amount of tofu and bean sprout casserole she could get away with. Halfway through dinner, the phone rang. Muttering that people had no manners anymore, her dad got up to answer it. Morgan's ears perked up a moment later at the sharp rise in her dad's voice.

"When did that happen?" His words were crisp. "What hospital did the ambulance go to?"

Morgan gasped.

"Jacob!" her mom cried, jumping up and running to the phone.

Morgan and Maya froze, staring at each other. Morgan barely breathed.

"Yes, thank you for calling," her dad finally said. "Tell her not to worry about anything. We'll figure something out."

Her?

"What was that about?" Maya asked as her parents came back to the table.

"Mrs. Delaney, the woman who was going to run the Gnosh for me next week. She fell this afternoon from her garage roof—"

"Garage roof!" Maya cried.

Mr. Cross nodded. "She'd been helping her husband replace shingles. That was him on the phone. She broke one leg, and the other leg has a hairline fracture. She won't be able to help us out next week at all." He slapped his hand palm-down on the table, making the glasses jump. "That would figure! I was counting on her, too. She knew the ropes, moved twice as fast, and did twice the work of most servers."

"But we're all leaving for New York in the morning," Maya said. "Will you just close the Gnosh next week?"

"Amber and Jamie can't run it alone," their dad agreed. "Amber's brand-new at this. Even with Benny to prep the food and cook, we need more help out front."

"And cleaning up," Mrs. Cross added. "You know Benny won't touch a dirty dish or sweep a floor."

Mr. Cross shook his head slowly. "I can't afford to close the restaurant for an entire week."

"But you have to attend that management seminar to keep your license," Mrs. Cross said.

"True. Even if we just kept the restaurant open during the breakfast and lunch crowds, and closed at five or so, that would be enough." He looked from Maya to Morgan, and then back at Maya again.

"Don't look at me like that," Maya said. "I can't stay home and work. I have those colleges lined up to look at next week."

"I know." Her father paused. "But you don't actually have to be in New York for a school visit till Tuesday. You could run the Gnosh Pit this weekend, then fly in on Monday."

"Daa-aad!" Maya moaned. "No fair! Can't Morgan do it? She knows the restaurant as well as I do, and she doesn't have to be in New York for anything. She could stay behind."

"But I have somewhere to visit in New York, too!"

"Hold it." Their dad rubbed a hand wearily across his eyes. "If Jacob hadn't left already, I'd make him stay behind and work, but he's already on his way to Florida. And I won't let your mom miss this chance to meet that big gallery owner and maybe sell some of her work. So the bottom line is this: I need your help, girls."

Both girls stared grimly at their father.

"Maya, you can work here this weekend, then fly in and meet us on Monday. It'll probably cost $50 to change your ticket, but that's well worth it for the weekend business."

"What about me?" Morgan asked.

Her dad sighed, looked at his wife, and then sighed again. "I don't see a choice here. Morgan, I need you to stay and keep the business open next week."

Stunned, Morgan sat with her mouth hanging open. She couldn't believe it. How could they leave without her?

"We hate for you not to join us. But Maya has to see those schools. And we'll need another pair of reliable hands at the restaurant."

Morgan struggled to keep from crying. "So I'll stay here by myself?"

"Of course not," her mom said. "Since Alex will be in Texas, I could call Jamie's mother and ask if you can stay there for the week. We'll make it up to you, sweetie. Honest."

Morgan mechanically put down her fork and slumped back in her seat. This was the absolute pits. The pit of the pits. Maya always got special favors—Mom's car, more money even though she didn't work as hard as Morgan—but this was too much.

Besides, she knew her parents weren't just going to New York for that seminar and gallery meeting. They were talking about moving back there, and Morgan would be expected to uproot herself from her life in Edgewood with no thought for her feelings at all.

"I understand," Morgan forced out. "I'm going to my room." She slowly left the dining room and headed upstairs. She needed somebody to talk to. Desperately. And obviously no one in her family cared how she felt. She brightened slightly at the sight of her computer. GlobalBuddies were so much easier. And on the Net, somebody actually cared.

chapter.4

Morgan took her laptop down to the den and logged on, using the family phone line. She didn't care if she tied it up. Nobody cared about *her* feelings obviously. Soon she'd blotted her family from her mind as she logged on to GlobalBuddies.com. Great! Last_wish was there. Looked like he was sharing his struggles with the cancer.

jellybean14: U R dying? 4 real??

last_wish: yeah. they've tried surgery & chemo. not much left 2 try.

NYGuy4u: man, that's a total drag.

timberwolf: my uncle died last year from the Big C. tuff 2 beat.

jellybean14: U can always talk 2 us. we want 2 B your friends.

last_wish: would b nice 2 have good friends. i spend so much time in the hosp. that i'm not 2 close 2 my friends anymore. at least my mom is cool. we're real close.

jellybean14: howz she doing? I mean . . . U really think U won't get well?

last_wish: it's like . . . i can handle the meds, the pain. what kills me is seeing my mom. my dad left when i was little. i'm sorta all she has.

jellybean14: there's still hope though.

last_wish: nope, ran fresh out of hope. i'm gonna die. i'm not afraid of that. i'm just afraid 2 leave my mom. she works so hard—two jobs—trying 2 pay hosp bills. she's worn out. me 2.

jellybean14: i know u have 2 go rest. i'll check on u tomorrow.

last_wish: C U then. thanks.

Morgan twisted in her chair and glanced out a den window, surprised to see that it was already dark. Looking at the clock, she realized that she'd been talking to last_wish so long that she'd spaced out the TodaysGirls chat for the night. None of them had Instant Messaged her a reminder either, even though they could see she was online. She figured everyone was still mad at her for losing the biggest swim meet of the season. Well, what difference did it make? She was helping a boy who was dying. It made her own hurt feelings seem totally petty.

Out in the hallway, Morgan noticed how quiet the house

was. Her parents were packing for their trip. Jacob had left for Florida already. And Maya wasn't speaking to her because of Darryl. She might as well return to the Net. There was always someone to talk to there.

An hour later, her mom padded barefoot into the den and sat on the arm of a chair. "It's about bedtime. You OK?"

"Yeah. Just talking to some kids whose problems are way worse than my not going to New York." Morgan watched the conversation flow onto the screen. "I still need to check my Save the Seals bulletin board again. I didn't realize how many kinds of seals all around the world are endangered."

"I love what you're doing. You've always had a kind heart." Mom glanced at the active computer screen. A smile grew on her face. "Remember when you were six and you tried to revive that dead squirrel out in the street?"

"Oh, yeah." Morgan giggled. "What was I thinking?"

Her mom laughed, too. "You kept waving acorns in front of its nose, telling it to wake up and eat something, then it would be OK." She patted Morgan's shoulder. "Just don't forget about yourself, honey. Get some sleep."

"I'll get off soon, Mom."

"All right. I talked to Janet Chandler, and she's thrilled that you can stay with them next week. Remember, your dad and I will be leaving for the airport *very* early tomorrow."

"Yeah, and without *me.*"

"I'm so sorry it worked out this way. But we'll call every

night. You'll probably get sick of us. We also want to take you on a special trip once school is out." She got up to leave. "Oh! I almost forgot. The art gallery is supposed to call. They'll leave a message for me about my appointment with the owner to show my work. Be sure to leave the answering machine on, and stay off the family phone line so they can get through."

"I will. I'll use our teen line. Oh, and don't worry about the Gnosh Pit. I've got it covered."

"I'm very proud of you, Morgan Lucille."

"Don't ruin it by calling me that."

"See you in the morning then." Mom bent to kiss Morgan's cheek. "Don't be too long now."

"'Night. I won't."

Morgan didn't even look at the clock when she finally stretched and logged off. She didn't want to know how late it was.

"Good morning, you sleepy cyber head." Dad shook Morgan's covered feet. "We're leaving for the airport. Listen to me. Are you awake?"

"Mmmph," Morgan grunted before rolling over.

"Listen. It's important. Remember what we told you. The art gallery will call for your mother about the show. And we'll call often, here and at Jamie's. We love you."

"Love you, too. Good night."

"Good *morning*, Jellybean," Dad poked her side, and then he was gone.

As Morgan lay there, listening to the sound of her parents driving away, she realized that Alex had also left for Texas at 6:30 A.M. on a bus and had never called to say good-bye. That wasn't like her. Was she mad, too?

The house was sure quiet. Her parents were gone. Jacob was gone. Alex was gone. And where was Maya? Morgan sat up, groggy. She decided to get some orange juice and clear the cobwebs out of her head. She grabbed her laptop out of the den on her way.

When Morgan reached the kitchen, she spotted a note in the middle of the island. "I'm @ Gnosh. If all you're going to do is surf the Net, come to work. Maya."

Morgan grabbed a banana and some juice before plugging her laptop into the teen line's phone jack. She had to check on last_wish before she did anything else. She sat back, soothed by the familiar pattern of clicks and whirs. She felt like they were waking up together to face the day.

She clicked her e-mail icon and watched it load thirteen pieces of mail! And only two pieces were junk mail. Obviously, not *everyone* had abandoned her. She had eleven messages to read and respond to. Friends were waiting to hear from her! *This rocks*, she thought silently.

Morgan first clicked on the e-mail from ANNA:

Jellybean, I took your advice and talked to my mom about her not worrying so much about my eating, but it didn't really help. Now she's MEASURING my food and writing down every-thing I eat! And get this! She says I have an eating disorder because I'm obsessed with food! She's the one obsessed with my eating habits and making me think about food 24/7. I don't know what to do anymore. My dad even got in on the act. I can't deal with both of them doing this to me.

Morgan hit *Reply* and wrote:

Dear ANNA, I'm sorry your parents are on your case even worse. It sounds to me like it's your mother who is obsessed. Maybe she doesn't have enough to do. My mom has hobbies and teaches. Maybe you could help your mom find some-thing better to do with her time, put her focus somewhere else. Then she might leave you alone. Good luck —Jellybean

Just then, someone pounded on the back door, making Morgan slosh orange juice in her lap. "Good grief," she mut-tered, dabbing at her T-shirt with a dishcloth. She opened the back door to find Jared on the step, his hand raised to pound again.

"OK! I'm here!" Morgan exclaimed. "You were loud enough to wake the dead."

"I wondered if I would have to do just that." He stomped into the kitchen. "I see you're not dead."

"Why would I be?"

"There had to be some reason why you didn't show up last night."

"Oh!" Morgan gasped. "Jared, I'm sorry! I totally forgot."

"Where the heck were you? I called for two hours and couldn't get through." He turned when a quiet *ping!* announced that Morgan had more mail. "So *that's* what you were doing. What are you, some kind of chat room addict? You waste your time with fake friends while people in *real* life are waiting on you."

Morgan reached over and closed the mailbox. "That's not fair. I got some bad news last night. It's a long story, but I don't get to go to New York after all. My parents already left, but Maya isn't going till Monday." She proceeded to tell him about the woman who fell off the garage roof. "And since I can't go to the aquarium on Coney Island now, I started researching on-line last night for the project. I'm sorry I forgot the meeting." Morgan ignored the sick feeling in her stomach over the lie she'd just told her best guy friend in the world.

"No, *I'm* sorry," Jared said. "That's rotten luck about your trip. And I should never have called you an addict."

"It's OK. How about if the three of us meet this afternoon, like at three o'clock at the library? Will that work?"

"Yeah, and I'll call Ty. Say, did you send in the money to Adopt-A-Seal?"

Morgan paused. She'd forgotten that, too! "I mailed it this morning. I'll collect Ty's share this afternoon. We should get

47

something back next week, in plenty of time for our presentation." *Man, that was two lies in less than a minute,* Morgan thought. What was the matter with her? She'd totally spaced off the adoption thing, but she'd mail the money right away after Jared left. She remembered putting the money in the front of her geometry book. Luckily, she'd had a geometry assignment and brought the book home.

"See you at three then." Jared opened the kitchen door and ran right into Maya. "Hello, Magnificent Maya." He waved and bounded down the steps whistling.

Maya smiled briefly, and then wrinkled her nose in disgust. "Isn't that what you wore last night? Did you *sleep* in it?" She shook her head. "Since you're not doing anything, we need you down at the Gnosh. I only came home long enough to change my shoes. Fashionable is killing me," she said, kicking off her clogs.

"Um, sorry, but I can't go right now." Morgan glanced quickly at her laptop, then away. "I just told Jared I'd meet him and Ty at the library to work on our group project."

"Well you can just *un*-tell him!" Maya's index finger was just two inches from Morgan's nose. "Get yourself dressed right now. Five minutes. Then you're coming with me."

Morgan bit her lower lip. She couldn't go off and leave all those e-mails unanswered. She didn't want her friends to think she was neglecting them.

Wait. Idea!

"Fine, I'll work lunch, but I need to go to the library after the crowd thins out," Morgan said. "And you know, you don't have to order me around." She disconnected her laptop and took it with her when she went upstairs to get dressed. She buried it in her school bag under a couple of books to take to the library.

She was on the way out her bedroom door when she remembered the Adopt-A-Seal money. She grabbed her geometry book off her desk and shook it, but no money fell out. She shook it again then riffled through the pages. Nothing.

Oh no, what did I do with that money? Morgan hoisted her school bag to her shoulder. She'd gotten so spacey lately. It was getting harder and harder to hide.

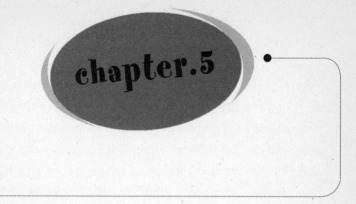

chapter.5

Morgan trudged into the Gnosh Pit on Saturday morning on the heels of Maya's running shoes. "I'll just dump my books in Dad's office, then I'll grab my order pad."

"Make it snappy."

Morgan saluted, but Maya had already headed to the kitchen, waving at several people already occupying booths. Morgan whipped into the office, bent to stash her bag under the desk, and then paused in mid-motion when she saw the phone jack. Sliding down the wall to a squatting position, Morgan made a quick decision. *I'll only take a minute*, she promised herself.

Unzipping her bag, she pulled out her freshly charged laptop, disconnected the office phone, and then plugged in her computer. She'd just check her most important mail, and then race to the counter to help. Right away, a message from ANNA caught her eye.

Help, jellybean! I took your advice and tried to get my mom interested in a hobby so she wouldn't have so much time to focus on me. I thought she might like to go on walks or bike rides with me, but she even turned THAT into an eating dis-order lecture! She claims it's just an excuse to burn off what few calories I consume. WHAT IS WRONG WITH THIS WOMAN? Now she wants me to see a counselor. I think SHE'S the one who needs help! Now what? ANNA

"Hey, Morgan, come on!" Jamie called. "Where are you?"

Morgan slid down farther behind her dad's desk and held her breath. Jamie walked past the office and knocked on the rest room door. "Hurry up in there!" she called. "We need you out front!"

Morgan waited till Jamie went back to waiting tables, then typed quickly:

ANNA, I've only got a minute, but I wanted you to know I got your message. I'm sorry about your mom! Talk about para-noid. Well, you tried. It's not your fault she didn't want to go on walks with you. It really does sound like your mom needs to see a counselor instead of you. Would your dad help her find someone to talk to? In the meantime, try to do your

walking or biking when she's not around, so she doesn't
worry. You're not doing anything wrong. Everybody exercises,
or least they should! Gotta run. Write back! Jellybean

Morgan left the rest of the messages in her in-box unanswered. She felt determined to help both last_wish and ANNA,
but right now she needed to get out front before Maya came and
dragged her out by her hair.

Morgan paused at the cash register to grab a pencil and order
pad, then moved next to Jamie. "OK, I'm set. Which tables are
mine?"

"If you'll take the booths along the window, Maya and I can
handle the tables." She peered closely at Morgan. "You OK? You
were in the rest room a long time."

Morgan nodded, but rubbed her stomach. "Must have eaten
something that didn't agree with me, but I'm fine now."

"Good! We need you!" Jamie rolled her eyes. "Just look out
for Benny this morning. He's on the warpath about something."

Oh great, Morgan thought, *that's all we need.* Even in his best
moods, their gruff cook, Benny, was as sour as old grapes, as her
mom said. He came in early every day to prepare the food, mix-
ing salads and baking pastries and muffins. Then he stayed to
cook up the orders since none of them were legally old enough to
cook yet. Benny rarely said more than ten words in a whole day,
most of them being variations of "get out of my way!"

Morgan moved to the first booth at the window and started

taking orders. The jumping preschoolers wanted blueberry pancakes and their mom a mushroom omelet. Morgan nodded,
smiled, and wrote their order, all the time thinking about
ANNA and last_wish. If only she could help more. They seemed
to be counting on her.

In the kitchen, she handed her order to Benny, and then
hurried back to the second booth of junior high kids, then the
third booth of three jocks in baseball caps turned backward.
After taking orders for all the booths, Morgan glanced over her
shoulder, and then raced back to the office. She was still
plugged into the phone line, and she logged on quickly to
GlobalBuddies.com. Eagerly she scanned the names of the
people in the room, spotting last_wish near the bottom of the
list.

She clicked on "private message" and began writing.

jellybean14: Hi! I'm @ the restaurant helping out. It's a real
bummer, but I have 2 stay home and help run things
while my family heads off to New York. But I was thinking. How about if I put a big box or can by the cash register with a sign asking 4 donations 4 U and UR mom?

last__wish: that is so awesome! are U sure it's ok?

jellybean14: sure, my dad won't mind. We have a March of
Dimes donation box. Actually, 2 get more people involved,
I could just ask lots of people to send $$

last__wish: it's great that U care so much. but my mom

wouldn't go 4 either idea. last fall i said we should ask 4 help, right after my dad split.

jellybean14: your dad left?

last_wish: yeah, he said he couldn't stay & watch me die. anyway, mom started working double shifts @ the factory, which is killing her. i'm worried about her. i asked her if i could ask 4 cards 2 B sent 2 us & if people would just include $1. i thought if we got enough cards that my mom wouldn't have 2 work so hard 2 pay the doctor bills

jellybean14: that was a great idea!

last_wish: mom didn't think so. she said it was like begging, & we were NOT charity cases.

jellybean14: i can C her point. my parents would say the same thing.

But, Morgan thought suddenly, it wouldn't prevent *her* from posting the notices and asking for money on their behalf. Since no one would be home to collect their mail all during break, she could have all the cards and money sent to the restaurant. Then she'd send it anonymously, all at one time, to last_wish and his mom. Morgan grinned just thinking about it.

But her grin disappeared a moment later. "Morgan! Get out here!" Maya yelled. "Your food's ready!"

Morgan quickly signed off, and then raced out front. Several of her orders were sitting under the warming lamps.

"You sure you're OK?" Jamie asked, worry lines forming between her eyebrows. "If you're sick, you should go home. You haven't been yourself for days, ever since the meet actually."

Morgan felt guilty over her concern. "I'm really OK." She grabbed the three warm breakfast plates and hurried to the first booth. She set the mushroom omelet in front of the young mother, then the matching meals in front of her bouncing children. "Can I get you anything else?" she asked.

"Mom!" the little boy yelled, yanking on his mother's sleeve. "I wanted pancakes! Where's my blueberry pancakes?"

"I wanted pancakes, too!" cried the girl in pigtails.

Morgan looked down at her order. She'd written two orders of blueberry *muffins,* and that's what she'd given them. Yet . . . something in the back of her mind echoed that these kids *had* ordered pancakes. They were raising such a ruckus that Maya came over.

"Need some help?"

"No, I just—" Morgan began.

"We asked for pancakes! Where's our pancakes?" the girl cried.

"I'm sorry," Morgan said to the woman. "I'll be right back with those blueberry pancakes." She took the muffins and headed to the kitchen, but not before she saw Maya roll her eyes.

Morgan worked hard to keep her mind on her job for the next couple of hours, but she found herself spacing out as she imagined the look on last_wish's face when the hundreds of dollars—or even thousands—arrived from her in the mail!

On Saturday night, Morgan actually looked forward to the group chat in the evening. Even though Maya had been snippy with her all the way to the bank and home, Jamie had been really nice.

When she entered the TodaysGirls.com site, Morgan read Amber's next Thought for the Day for Easter week:

For God loved the world so much that he gave his only Son. God gave his Son so that whoever believes in him may not be lost, but have eternal life. John 3:16
  Can you imagine love that BIG? What a sacrifice God made for us! Awesome!

Even though she believed God did it, Morgan couldn't imagine letting a child of hers die for anyone. Why did it have to be that way?

Morgan typed in her alias and password, and then joined her friends in their private chat room.

rembrandt: cool passage, Amber
faithful1: thanx. good 4 Easter
jellybean: I like Easter ok. but wouldn't it B a much better story if Jesus didn't die? it's so morbid
nycbutterfly: duh . . . sort of the point of the thing
faithful1: it WAS morbid, M. but Jesus had 2 die, 2 save us. something really good came out of something really bad.

chicChick: i'm here. Sorry i'm L8. i've just been so busy, it's been so exciting! i'm back in my hotel room now. U should see the furniture.

TX2step: hi y'all from afar!

jellybean: U made it to Texas!

TX2step: left @ 6 this mornin' & got 2 TX @ 7 tonight. majorly boring bus ride.

chicChick: well WE just went 2 the kewlest restaurant. overlooked the river. cutest waiters! they had towels over their arms and everything! most of them spoke english. their accents are so attractive.

rembrandt: liking paris, then? sounds like it.

chicChick: no. LUVing it.

rembrandt: I would luv all the art!

chicChick: going 2 the louvre tomorrow, Jamie. i'll get a postcard or a print of some painting 4 U. this is such a beautiful, romantic city! wish you guyz were here!!!

jellybean: howz texas, Alex?

TX2step: good, but R computer is down. lightning storm blasted it. I'm on @ library. otherwise, fine

jellybean: good thing some of U will B having fun. i'll B @ the Gnosh all week U know . . . so my sis can do the city. so much 4 saving the seals!

nycbutterfly: as if U even like the city

faithful1: hey, I'll make sure we have a blast this week

jellybean: doing what? the dishes?

faithful1: ha! it's the holiday! maya & morgan--come 2 Palm Sunday services with me tomorrow, ok?
nycbutterfly: U got a deal
jellybean: OK, me 2

Morgan yawned as Bren gave a long-winded account of some French waiter who wanted to take her dancing, and Morgan's mind wandered to last_wish's financial condition since his father abandoned them. If only she could help more! If only—

Then it hit her. The idea was downright brilliant. She could post ads on bulletin boards in charity Web sites, asking for cards with dollar bills inside for last_wish. She could get *some* money from the Gnosh, but this would get the word out much faster. She'd have the cards sent c/o the restaurant. When she had a big chunk, she'd mail them to last_wish and his mom! What a surprise *that* would be.

Morgan whipped into her pajamas, excited by her idea. She might be a lousy server, but she really cared about people. Hair pulled up in back, Morgan hunched over her computer and got to work. She hit charity Web sites. Nonprofit organizations. Teen sites. Cancer support groups. Everything she could think of. Her message about last_wish and his mom was touching, but not pushy. Single-handedly, she would make the boy's dream come true.

Hours later Morgan blinked several times, but her vision stayed blurry. She rubbed and kneaded the goose-egg knots on the back of her neck. She turned off the computer and headed to bed after swallowing a couple of aspirin for her ripping headache.

It was only as she lay down in the welcome dark that she remembered. Jared and Ty! They'd been waiting for her at the library again that afternoon! Even if they'd tried to call and remind her, she'd kept the Gnosh's phone line tied up, then was online after she came home.

Morgan pounded her pillow with her fist. No matter how she tried, lately her life was one long string of broken promises.

chapter.6

"Morgan, I've called you three times." Morgan felt the swoosh of cold air as her covers were ripped off her. "Come on!"

"Maya!" Morgan reached to pull back the blankets.

"We both told Amber we'd go to Palm Sunday services with her. You have half an hour. Move your carcass."

Morgan thought about Amber for a minute. She *had* promised her, but she was so beat.

"I can't, Maya. Tell Amber I'm too tired."

"Fine, but if you're going to dog Amber and stay home, get off your duff and do your chores. It's a total pit in here."

"Sure. Whatever," she added under her breath. Morgan burrowed her head under her pillow until Maya left, and then stayed in bed till she heard the chugging motor of Mr. Beep pulling out of the drive. Yawning, she dragged herself out of bed and headed down the hall to Maya's room.

She immediately spotted the note taped to the computer monitor. A deep anger welled up inside as Morgan read, "Don't you dare stop this downloading or unhook our line. I have to take this stuff to NYC with me. Maya."

Morgan checked the volume of material that Maya was downloading and knew it would take forever. She wouldn't be able to use that phone line for ages. Fuming, she stormed down to the kitchen and grabbed a box of Frosted Flakes left sitting on the counter. She munched her way through a handful, tempted to interrupt Maya's download. Maya would kill her, but what else could Morgan do? She was forbidden to tie up the other phone line so Mom's gallery call could get through.

While crunching through her second handful, the family phone rang. "Hello." Morgan choked on her dry cereal.

"Well someone woke up with a frog in her throat," Dad said. "Anything wrong, sweetie?"

"Hi, Daddy. Nothing. I just had my mouth full." She paused. "Well, actually, Maya's being a pain. She downloaded like two tons of college stuff. It's gonna be printing out until my seventeenth birthday." She paused. "She didn't even *ask* or *anything*. And now the phone line is tied up. *Again*."

"Honey, tell me the truth, were you on the computer last night?"

"Well, yes."

"For hours?"

"Well, yeah, but—"

"So it's not really as unfair as you think, is it? And we do need that information for the college visits, so don't stop the download."

Then her mom took the phone. "Honey, remember to leave this line open in case the gallery calls. The call has to come today because the owner said I'd hear from him this weekend."

"Why don't you just call him from your hotel?" Morgan asked. "It wouldn't even be long distance."

"Because he said not to, that he'd be in and out all weekend."

"OK, Mom." Morgan felt her frustration build. Everyone got to use the phone lines except her, and *she* was the one being left behind! Her mom wasn't even in town and she'd called dibs on the family line.

"Oh, and tell Maya that Amber is to make the night deposits with the restaurant money each evening. Also, since Amber can't work late the Saturday before Easter, Dad will let you know where to keep the money overnight. Then he'll deposit it Easter evening when we get home. OK?"

"Yeah, I got it. I'll tell Maya."

"OK. Love you."

Morgan hung up the phone and stared at the receiver. She wanted to stop Maya's download. It was true that she got to surf sometimes. But Maya always decided when, and for how long. Maya used it for every TodaysGirls chat. For homework. College research. And now she'd have it all morning, even though she was at church. If Morgan interrupted the download, she'd get caught for sure. And it wasn't like Morgan could use the other line.

Or could she?

All she wanted to do was check for important messages. There could be some news about last_wish's money. ANNA needed support, too. What if someone was waiting for her to write? Checking her e-mail wouldn't take more than a minute or two. Anyway, what gallery owner would call so early on a Sunday morning?

Morgan ran to her room for her laptop, then came back and unplugged the phone. The first message she read when she logged on was from ANNA, and she sounded desperate.

Jellybean: I found my mom reading my diary today! She's actually spying on me now! How can I convince her to lay off? How can I prove I don't have an eating disorder? I'm just naturally petite. If something doesn't improve SOON, I'm leaving home. Enuf is enuf! Help me!! –ANNA

Morgan twirled a chunk of hair around her finger as she studied ANNA's note. How *could* ANNA prove she didn't have an eating disorder? Were there actual symptoms? Or blood tests she could take? Morgan clicked over to her favorite search engine, Ask Jeeves.com, and wrote: "Where can I learn about eating disorders?"

In just seconds, Morgan had a list of more than two dozen sites. At the first one, she learned from Overeaters Anonymous that they felt the problem should be turned over to a Higher Power for help, whatever the heck that meant.

Three sites later, though, Morgan found what she was looking for at eating-disorders.com. "Do you have an eating disorder?" was the title of the questionnaire. Morgan grabbed a pencil and paper to make notes. Then she could direct ANNA—and her mom, if she'd be willing to learn about it—to this site for more information. Surely, then ANNA's mom would realize she needed to cool it and not push her daughter over the edge.

Pencil poised, Morgan read through the list of questions. *Do you worry about gaining weight? Are you preoccupied with losing weight? Do you frequently diet?* Those questions sounded straightforward, Morgan thought, and easy to answer. However, when she read the rest of the list, a few questions made her squirm for some reason, almost as if they applied to her! But that couldn't be, Morgan rationalized. She'd never wanted to diet. Still, the questions bothered her for some reason. *Do you use food to comfort yourself? At times do you feel as if you have lost control? Do you spend a significant amount of time thinking about when you will get to eat next? Do you try to hide how much you eat?*

When she finished making notes, she e-mailed ANNA and told her about the eating disorder Web sites:

OK, ANNA, from what you've told me, you wouldn't answer "yes" to hardly any of these questions. Show your mom the list and your score—if you take their test. Then whether she agrees or not, just try to tune her out and live your life. As time passes, she'll see that she had absolutely nothing to worry about. Hope these web sites are useful! –jellybean J

Morgan poured herself a glass of milk, and then quickly checked the rest of her e-mail. She had seven new messages already from people writing about last_wish! So Morgan dived into responding to the e-mails, thanking those who'd written. Two people suggested other sites where Morgan could post messages, like TeensHelpingTeens.com, where she found a dozen more links to similar sites.

The last e-mail was from ANNA, a quick "thank you" for the web site information:

J'BEAN: I checked it out and you were 100% right! I just KNEW I didn't have a problem. You're a life saver! –ANNA

Morgan grinned. Suddenly it didn't matter so much that her parents were in New York and her brother in Florida and Alex in Texas. She had friends! They really cared about her and appreciated her help. And if need be, she could take them with her if she ended up moving to the Big Apple.

Without warning, Morgan heard the chugging sound of Mr.

Beep in the drive. Panicky, Morgan glanced at the kitchen clock. She was back from church already! Maya would squeal on her for sure. Morgan hurriedly unplugged the laptop and hid her computer in the den, then raced back to try to reconnect the answering machine—just as Maya walked in the kitchen door.

"You're still in your pajamas?" Maya waved a palm branch as she entered the kitchen.

Morgan inched around to block her sister's view of the unattached cord. "How was church? Are you hungry? I can get you something. Do you need help packing?"

"Why are you being so nice? Did you halt my download?"

"No, I didn't. I promise. I just figured you'd be in a hurry to pack. Do you need to put in some last-minute laundry?" Morgan pointed Maya toward the basement stairs.

"No. I'm all set. What's *with* you?" Morgan stared suspiciously at her little sister.

"Nothing." She leaned casually against the counter, crossing one leg over the other, continuing to block Maya's view of the answering machine. "Oh, Mom and Dad called about the money at the restaurant. They said—"

She was interrupted as the family phone behind her rang. Morgan turned around to answer it, but Maya yelled, "Don't!"

"Why not?"

"I just know it's Darryl, and I don't want to talk to him. He's probably been trying our teen line all morning. Just let the answering machine get it." Maya left the kitchen in a huff.

Morgan held her breath as the phone rang twice, then three times. In another ring, when the disconnected answering machine didn't click on, Maya would know she'd been online that morning. At the beginning of the fourth ring, Morgan grabbed the phone.

"Hello?"

"Hi, again. Long time no chitchat," said her mom. "Is Maya home yet?"

"Yes. She just got home. We'll probably eat lunch soon, then she's going to pack . . ." While talking, Morgan quietly plugged the answering machine back in.

"Did the gallery call, sweetie? Were there *any* messages?"

"Um, no. No calls. I'm sorry." Thank goodness her mom hadn't tried to call home ten minutes ago!

"I don't understand it." The disappointment was thick in her mother's voice. "The owner sounded so interested when we talked last week. Maybe I should have called him anyway. I don't know . . ."

Morgan's stomach lurched as if she might be sick, and she wanted off the phone. "Let me get Maya," she said.

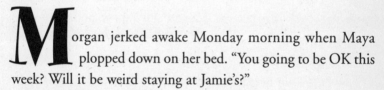

chapter.7

Morgan jerked awake Monday morning when Maya plopped down on her bed. "You going to be OK this week? Will it be weird staying at Jamie's?"

"Wh—What?" Morgan groaned when she saw the clock. She'd only gotten to bed four hours before. "I guess it'll be OK." Morgan struggled to sit up and wrapped her arms around her knees. "What time is Coach coming?"

"In half an hour, so I can get to the airport an hour before the flight."

"Are you scared flying alone?"

Maya shrugged. "I might have been if I had to change planes in Chicago, but it's just three hours nonstop to La Guardia." She pulled out Morgan's already loose hair band. "Better get dressed. He's dropping you and Jamie off at the Gnosh after taking me."

Maya got up and headed for the door. "I'm sorry you'll be working this week while I tour New York. I know that wasn't the plan."

"It's not your fault, and I'll earn some extra cash. I know you guys will call."

Maya stopped abruptly. "Speaking of which, did Mom ever get that call from the gallery? I never took a message."

"Me either." Morgan looked away. Well, that was *true*. She threw back the sheets and stretched her legs.

"Hmm. Well, I'm going to finish getting ready." And with that, Maya disappeared.

Maya's awfully friendly this morning, Morgan thought. *Must be excited about leaving today.* Morgan got a move on because she needed to quickly check her e-mail. What if ANNA or last_wish was trying to reach her?

She pulled on her clothes, washed her face, and brushed her teeth, then stuffed her midsized suitcase with enough clothes to last a week. Morgan was heading to the kitchen with her laptop when a horn honked.

"There's Coach," Maya called. "You ready?"

Oh, shoot! Morgan half groaned. She was just getting ready to check her e-mail.

"Yes! I'm coming!" answered Morgan.

She ran back upstairs and packed her computer into her backpack. There could be messages about the money for last_wish. Hopefully Alex had written, too. She'd been strangely quiet during the chat the other night. Was she mad at Morgan, or were her parents having trouble like before? It was their problems that had forced Alex to Edgewood to live with her grandparents in the first place.

Morgan grabbed her suitcase with one hand and her backpack with the other, then headed downstairs and out to Coach's waiting van.

An hour later, they had dropped Maya at the TWA entrance for her 7:00 A.M. flight. Morgan hugged her hard before watching her stroll into the terminal, her luggage rolling along behind her. On the way back to Edgewood, Jamie turned to face Morgan in the backseat while pulling her hair into a ponytail.

"How busy do you think we'll be today?"

"Monday mornings are usually light, Dad said."

"But this is the first day of spring break. You think tons of kids will come in?"

"I hadn't thought of that." Panic suddenly rose in Morgan. What if they were swamped with kids on break? Then she'd never get a chance to check her mail! Morgan decided that she couldn't stand it any longer. She had to get online. "Coach, could you drop me off at Jamie's house? I've got my clothes for the week with me. You can take Jamie to the Gnosh—I'll give her my key to get in—and I'll just walk over."

"Sure, I'll stop at Jamie's, but we can wait while you unload your stuff."

"No. It's not a long walk at all."

"Nonsense. We'll wait for you."

Morgan frowned a moment, then she brightened. She could use her dad's office phone to get online! "On second thought, go directly to the Gnosh. I'll stash my stuff in Dad's office and take it home after work."

Amber was waiting out front when they pulled up, and Morgan quickly unlocked the front door and flipped on the overhead lights. She waited till Jamie and Amber followed her inside, and then relocked the door. Benny would have been there an hour already, prepping food for the day. Morgan could hear him banging around and slamming cupboard doors in the kitchen. They always stayed out of Benny's way in the morning. With just twenty minutes before the breakfast crowd descended at eight, Amber and Jamie grabbed silverware and began setting tables.

"I'll be right back," Morgan called after them. "I'm sticking my suitcases in Dad's office."

A moment later, she closed the office door, unzipped her backpack, pulled out her laptop, and hooked it into the restaurant's phone jack—all in one fluid motion. In just two minutes, she was online and watching eighteen e-mails load!

Morgan's excitement grew as the numbers climbed. If only she had time to go through all the messages right then. She scrolled down; fourteen of them said "Re: last_wish donation" in the subject line. Excellent! She quickly e-mailed last_wish to say "hi" and that she was busy working that morning, but would get back to him later that day. How she wished she could tell him about her secret plan and the results coming in already. Oh well, the time would come for that soon.

She clicked over to her TodaysGirls.com in-box and spotted an e-mail from Alex with SUPER PRIVATE!!!! in the subject line. What in the world . . .?

Morgan's heart went out to Alex when she read the e-mail. No wonder she'd been quiet in the chat room the other night. She'd written:

Morgan--
Don't even hint to anyone, including Maya, what's really going on. My dad and mom had this huge knock-down fight cuz my dad lost his job again. He didn't show up for work three days in a row. We aren't going to Padre Island, but DON'T TELL ANYONE! Meet me in TG.com to private chat this morning at ten. i'm logging on at the library. Lightning didn't fry our computer--our phone got cut off. Please be there!
--Alex

Morgan hit *Reply* and said:

Alex--
I'm so sorry what's going on down there. I'm at the Gnosh right now, but ten should be OK. Breakfast rush will be over. Hang in there! See you later. Hugs to you.
--Morgan

"Morgan, time to roll! It's eight o'clock," Jamie called. "I'm opening up!"

"Coming!" Morgan shut things down momentarily and reconnected the Gnosh phone line.

The next two hours passed in a dizzy blur. Besides the regular people for breakfast—like the retired folks and the people who didn't have to be at the office until nine—they did have an overflow crowd of students on vacation. Morgan shook her head in disbelief as they jammed all ten booths. If *she* didn't have to work, she'd be home in bed asleep. She shook her head to clear away the fog, forced herself to smile, then took more orders.

At nine-thirty a group of girls two grades ahead of Morgan came in. Morgan seated them in booth number five by the window. She knew they were in the popular group, but they hadn't a clue who *she* was.

Morgan brought three ice waters and set them in the middle of the table, then flipped her order pad to a clean page. She waited, but it was like she was invisible.

"Brunch is just what we need to kick off our shopping day!" gushed the blonde with freckles.

"Don't you just love spring sidewalk sales?" a girl named Misty said. "I mean, American Eagle and the Gap have stuff 75 percent off! And I need some new sandals, too."

"Hey," said the third girl, glancing up from her menu. "Let's go to that new Matt Damon movie when we're shopped out, OK? It's playing at the mall, isn't it?"

"Yeah, it is—let's go while we're there. I just got my pay-check, so I've got money to blow! I saw that preview! Isn't he so cute?" the blonde asked, a longing look in her eyes.

Morgan cleared her throat. "Are you ready to order, or do you need a few more minutes?" she asked, trying to hide her jealousy. Instead of spending money and having a blast during her own vacation, she was stuck working, without even a license or car to attempt having some fun after hours.

They were ready to order, and Morgan wrote quickly. "That's three breakfast specials with pancakes coming in a few minutes," she said, leaving the juniors to their fun and trudging off to the kitchen.

As ten o'clock approached, Morgan kept a sharp eye on the clock. At 9:55, she took one last look at her booths, and then decided the dirty dishes could wait a minute. The breakfast crowd was thin, and the lunch crowd wouldn't arrive till nearly eleven. Giving tickets to the last three groups in her booths, Morgan scanned the restaurant to make sure her friends were busy, then snuck down the hallway to her dad's office and logged on.

Welcome to TodaysGirls.com! loaded in bright purple and magenta. She skipped past Amber's Thought for the Day and clicked to create a private chat. Alex wasn't there yet, but it was still one minute before ten.

Morgan tapped her fingernails on the desk, drumming a steady rhythm. *Come on, Alex, I don't have much time,* she thought, one ear alert for sounds from out front. She had three booths yet to bus, and she ought to be washing dishes in the kitchen to get ready for lunch.

While waiting, she clicked Amber's Thought for the Day open again:

All people have sinned and are not good enough for God's glory. People are made right with God by his grace, which is a free gift. They are made right with God by being made free from sin through Jesus Christ. Romans 3:23-24

Got freedom? When you think about yourself, are you free? I mean really free? Do it God's way!

Freedom? Morgan shook her head. When was the last time she'd felt free? She yawned widely, leaned her chin on her palm, and closed her eyes wearily. If only she could take a nap. Three minutes passed, then five, then six. *Alex, where are you?* she worried.

Just then, Morgan heard footsteps coming down the hall. She ducked as Jamie raced by the door on the way to the rest room, but she wasn't fast enough. Jamie halted in her tracks and stared open-mouthed into the office. "You're *online*? Please! We're swamped out there!" She hit her forehead with her open palm. "This is *your* family restaurant, you know."

"I'm coming," Morgan muttered, exiting the private chat room. *I'm sorry, Alex,* she said silently. "I'm sorry, Jamie," she said aloud. "It's just that—"

But Jamie had already disappeared, and Morgan heard the click of the rest room door locking. Morgan knew her soft-spoken friend had to be steamed to talk like that. Pressured by guilt, Morgan hurried out front.

She grabbed an empty dish tub and raced from booth to booth, stacking dirty dishes and cups into her plastic tub. The tips were surprisingly good for a Monday crowd, she thought as she scooped dollar bills into her apron pocket. On the way past the register, she added her tips to what was already filling the tip cup on the counter. At the Gnosh, everyone pooled their tips, and then split them equally at the end of the day. *I'd better not take any today,* Morgan thought, not after being caught online when she was supposed to be working.

Back in the kitchen, she rinsed her dishes and loaded the dishwasher. Benny stood at the center island, watching her from beneath bushy, unruly eyebrows, as he sliced croissants for sand-wiches. He wore very short white socks in worn leather loafers and khaki shorts year-round, showing broken blue veins on the back of his knees. He was no fashion plate, Morgan thought, but he was a great cook.

Just then, Jamie rushed in and set a dish tub full of dirty dishes on the counter.

"I'm sorry about being online a while ago," Morgan began.

"This is really getting out of hand and—"

"Wait!" Morgan interrupted. "I understand how you feel, but I wanted to tell you what I was checking." Just then,

Amber came into the kitchen with *another* load of dirty dishes. As they scraped and washed, Morgan filled them in on meeting last_wish and her desire to see him and his mom receive hundreds—even thousands—of cards with dollar bills in them.

"Oh, Morgan, that's sweet of you to care," Amber said, "but it could be a scam, don't you think?"

Benny grunted his agreement and twitched his gray-flecked mustache. Morgan's eyes opened wide. She'd expect that kind of reaction from their surly cook, but she was shocked that Amber wouldn't want to help last_wish.

"I don't understand," Morgan said quietly. "I mean it's not like it was his idea, not really. In fact, he didn't think it would work because his mom didn't want charity. She prefers working double shifts at some factory to pay the doctor bills."

"So you posted ads on bulletin boards about this without telling him?"

Morgan nodded eagerly. "I got fourteen responses already this morning. People really do care. And I want to put a dona-tion box out front."

Amber got quiet. "Well," she finally said, "I guess it can't hurt to set up a donation box by the register. Your dad does that sometimes for other causes." She opened two cupboard doors before she found the bright red box she was looking for. "Here. Put this by the register with a sign about last_wish."

"Thanks!"

"Hey," Jamie piped up, "we could donate part of our tips at the end of the day—that is, if everyone's willing."

"Really?" Morgan grinned at her friends. "I know that anything at all we can do will be appreciated. His dad left them when he got cancer, and if they had some financial help *now* his mom would be able to work just one shift and be home with her son—while he's still here."

Amber nodded. "We forget how blessed we are sometimes," she said. "If we can't help this boy and his family at Easter, when can we? But about being online, Morgan: This is work. So can you *please* not check your mail while stuff still needs to be done?"

Just then, the bell over the front door rang, and Morgan hurried out front, setting the red donation box by the cash register. Jared and Ty had just slid into a freshly cleaned booth where the table was still damp. "Hi, guys. Wuzzup?"

"That's what we'd like to know." Jared smiled, but his eyes were flashing. "Remember us?"

Tyler glanced up at Morgan, and then turned to study the salt and pepper shakers.

Just then, it hit her. "Oh, man, I'm sorry, you guys. Things were so busy Saturday I forgot about our meeting."

"*Again.*" Jared patted the pile of papers he'd laid on the table. "We went ahead and got some done, but we can only do so much when missing practically half the group. We don't want to do it all."

"You're right. I'm sorry," Morgan repeated. *Man, I spend half my life apologizing,* she thought. Every time she turned around, it seemed that she'd let another friend down.

"Luckily, we still have a week." Ty spoke for the first time. "If Muhammad won't come to the mountain, the mountain will come to Muhammad."

"What?" Morgan frowned.

"Nothing."

"Um, did you guys want to order lunch or anything?"

"Can't." Jared handed her a file folder full of papers. "I have to meet Coach in twenty minutes at the church. We're repainting some room in the basement to make a bigger nursery."

"I gotta go, too." Ty unfolded his gangly legs, slid out of the booth, and stood.

As they walked out, Morgan pointed to the donation box and told them what she planned. "Dump your loose change in here. I'm getting a basket set up today too, for the cards and money when they start coming in. Jamie even wants to donate some of our tip money," she said, nodding at the cup on the counter.

"I guess you have been busy," Jared admitted. "We'll call you to get together, for real this time."

"Sounds good. Sorry about forgetting again. Talk later." Morgan waved.

Around four o'clock, Coach pushed open the front door and trudged in, covered in paint splatters from the top of his thinning hair, down the front of the T-shirt barely covering his stomach, to where little drips had landed on his tennis shoes.

"Nursery get painted?" Morgan asked, setting a glass of water in front of him.

"How'd you know about that?"

"Jared was in before noon."

"Yup, we're done." He leaned back in the booth and heaved a loud sigh of relief. "Just wanted to let you know that when I got home, my wife said Maya had called to check in. She got to New York just fine."

"She called *you* instead?" Morgan was surprised how hurt she felt.

"She said she'd tried here for over an hour, but kept getting a busy signal." He looked at her quizzically. "Were you girls gabbing on the phone instead of working?"

Morgan blinked and pretended to be thinking. "No. No, I'm sure no one was talking on the phone." *But I forgot to reconnect the phone after trying to find Alex in the chat room this morning,* she thought. After taking Coach's order for a double-size fries, she pretended to go to the rest room, but dashed into her dad's office instead. In fifteen seconds, she had the phone reconnected. Sighing, she thought about Maya in New York. Her family suddenly seemed so very far away.

Later, after Coach left and they'd cleaned everything out front, Morgan convinced Jamie and Amber to go on home. Benny had left without a word an hour ago. "I'll stay and finish.

Since we're closing at five this week, I won't be late. I really don't mind." It was the least she could do after being online during work hours and leaving the phone disconnected all day. She just hoped they hadn't missed any other important phone calls.

Amber and Jamie finished wiping down the counter. "How much of our tips should we donate?" Jamie asked, reaching across the register for the cup of money. However, when she lifted it up, all that was left inside were a few pennies. "Where'd our tips go?" she asked. "Morgan, I said we could donate *part* of it to your dying friend, but I can't afford to donate it all."

"But I didn't take any yet," Morgan said, looking at the few cents. "Honest."

She turned toward Amber. "Don't look at me. I just put money *in* today. I didn't take it out." Amber and Jamie turned toward Morgan.

"Really, I didn't take it!" Morgan said.

The next few seconds passed in bewildered silence. Then Amber said, "We know you wouldn't. It's gotta be somewhere." She yawned and stretched. "In the meantime, I'm heading home. I've got the cash bag to deposit, in case your dad happens to ask. Coming, Jamie?"

Jamie nodded. "See you at home, Morgan. Thanks for closing." Morgan locked the door behind them when they left.

Only after Morgan watched Amber's car drive away did she remember the backpack and suitcase she was going to have to haul to Jamie's house. She groaned, but forced herself to begin refilling the sugar containers, then the salt and pepper shakers. She filled the silverware tub, restocked the glass case with candy and mints, and washed the large plate-glass window. Ignoring her pounding headache, she mopped the floor.

At last, Morgan stood in the middle of the deserted restaurant. All was silent. And she felt utterly, completely alone.

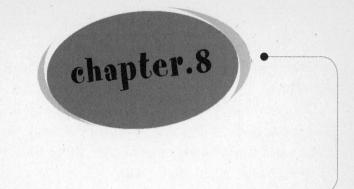

chapter.8

As soon as Morgan opened the door of the Gnosh on Tuesday morning, the noise of the breakfast rush hit her. It was only 8:30, but dishes and silverware already clattered. Voices blared. After being online answering questions about last_wish until 2:00 A.M., she'd given Jamie her key that morning to open up at 8:00. Already laughter erupted around the sunny room.

"Phew." Amber handed Morgan some silverware wrapped in paper napkins. "I was starting to get worried. Booth number eight needs setup." Amber swiped her forehead with the back of her hand, then ripped off a sheet from her order pad and handed it to Morgan without looking. "We've been swamped. I appreciate you closing last night, but please remember that I'm new to serving."

"Sorry." When Morgan turned, she spotted a familiar face in a booth. Coach waved her over.

"What's up?" Morgan asked while setting up the booth right behind him.

"That's my line." Coach pointed to the donation box and her sign that read: "Make a dying boy's last wish come true!"

"Oh, that. I'm collecting money to help a friend."

"What friend? Why?" asked Coach.

"I met a kid on the Net who has cancer. His screen name is last_wish because he's dying. They've tried everything, but even the chemo didn't work."

Coach Short drummed his stubby fingers on the table. "Honey, people can . . . well . . . alter the truth when writing online."

"I know, but he's not lying, Coach. I've gotten to know him. And he's worried about leaving his mom. It's just the two of them, so she'll be alone. She works double shifts, but his medical bills have left them broke."

"So you put up a donation box?" Coach asked.

"Plus I asked for cards. I want a million people to send cards and put one dollar inside each card—"

"A million dollars?" Coach roared. "You're trying to raise a million dollars for someone you met on the Internet?"

Morgan's eyes narrowed. "I'm surprised at you. You're a nice man. I thought you'd like the idea."

"Strangers won't send you money for some kid they don't

know," Coach said. "For that matter, they don't know *you* either. Anyway, he sounds like a con artist to me, Morgan."

"But he's not! It was *my* idea about the cards and money. It's going to be a surprise, to put his mind at ease about his mom when he dies." Irritated with herself, Morgan felt tears welling up. "I just want to help."

Coach just rolled his eyes.

Jamie stopped at Coach's booth. "Sorry to interrupt, but we need a roll of nickels and quarters, Morgan. Can you get it?"

"Sure." Glad to escape, Morgan slid out of the booth and raced to the office for more change from the metal box in the bottom desk drawer. She grabbed the money, shut the box, then couldn't resist quickly logging on. She just wanted to count the number of e-mails from people who'd promised to send her money and cards. *That* would give Coach an idea of how caring *most* people were about last_wish's condition.

She was still sorting and counting when Jamie rushed into the office. "Morg, do you have the—Morgan! We really need you to work right now." She pointed to the computer. "Please, can that wait?"

"Hey, Jamie." Amber popped her head into the office. "Where do we keep the children's menus?" She looked at Morgan. "What are you doing? It's filling up out there."

"I'm coming."

For the next hour Morgan waited on tables, chatting with the "regulars," always bringing the conversation around to her last_wish box. "I'm helping raise money for him and his family," she told customers. "So any spare change you could donate would be helpful."

"Could you please back off just a bit?" Jamie whispered when she and Morgan were behind the counter. "People will see the red box by the register. That's enough."

"All right. Well, since it's slowed down, I'm taking my break now. Alex wants to chat at ten."

"At least today Morgan's taking work breaks from her chatting." Amber winked at her. "That's progress."

"It's not that bad." Morgan headed to the office.

Hopefully Alex had received yesterday's e-mail and was waiting for her already. She pulled the desk chair close, switched the phone jack, and logged on. Clicking on her e-mail account, Morgan found twenty-one total messages! She scrolled down quickly.

Still no message from ANNA, Morgan noticed. She didn't want ANNA to think she'd forgotten her. She clicked on the New Message icon and wrote:

Long time since you wrote. You OK? I know it might be tough, but stand your ground with your mom. You're in charge of your own life!

Then Morgan clicked to the TodaysGirls.com Web site and read Amber's Thought for the Day:

Happy Easter week! We are so lucky!!

Jesus came here just for us . . . and all we have to do is believe that he died for our sins and accept him into our hearts. He is risen! So we can have new life!

Then, by believing, you can have life through his name. John 20:31

Morgan didn't understand most of the verses Amber posted, but a new life sure sounded inviting. Morgan pondered the meaning, and then clicked the chat icon.

TX2step: U there?

jellybean: yup. so what's been going on down there?

TX2step: i'm fit to be tied. big fights since dad lost another job. I hate the screaming so bad!

jellybean: did he, well . . .

TX2step: what?

jellybean: u no. hit anybody like before. r u OK?

TX2step: he just threw some stuff, but no one got hurt. I miss grandpa and grandma and my cat. I like peace and quiet more than I thought.

jellybean: i'm sorry! anything I can do?

Before Alex could answer, Amber called down the hall. "Morgan, please hurry! We need assistance!"

"Is the phone free?" Jamie added. "Benny needs to call for a bread delivery!"

> **jellybean: i'm sorry. Benny needs the phone.**
> **TX2step: food service duty. lucky U**
> **jellybean: sum1's gotta do it. hang in there!**
> **TX2step: no other choice. L8R**

Morgan closed the chat room. She started to log off the Internet, but decided to check her e-mail one last time . . . and finally a message had appeared in her in-box from ANNA! But when she began reading, her breath quickened and her fingers froze on the keyboard. The message wasn't from ANNA. It was from ANNA's mother:

Dear "jellybean," I know you have been writing to my daughter, Anna, and I thought you should know the damage you've done. Anna has been denying that she had an eating disorder for nearly a year, despite the fact that she is now under 85 pounds, her hair is falling out, she shivers constantly, and she never sleeps. She is literally starving herself to death before our very eyes. Before you first wrote to her, her counselor had finally gotten her to agree to hospitalization. Now, however, she is convinced (by you) that she's perfectly normal and her parents are the problem. She has refused to go into treatment now. Anna's in serious danger because you gave advice without knowing the whole situation. Please think twice before you do it again. Marilyn

Morgan sat motionless. Then her hands started trembling. *What in the world have I done?* What if ANNA died because of her? She'd only wanted to help, to be ANNA's friend! Mechanically, she logged off the Internet, shut down, and watched the screen go black. Something inside Morgan shut down at the same time.

chapter.9

Wednesday passed in a stunned blur as Morgan went about her restaurant duties, with the words of ANNA's mother replaying repeatedly in her head. She knew she needed to write back, but her mind wouldn't seem to function. She skipped the TodaysGirls.com chat that night and even neglected her other e-mail, including requests for information about last_wish.

The next morning, Morgan woke up on the Chandlers' couch and slapped at her alarm clock until it turned off. No light filtered through the drapes of the den. Four A.M.? Just for a minute, she couldn't remember why she was supposed to get up. The Gnosh didn't open for two hours. Then it hit her. She'd set her alarm to get up early Thursday morning to tackle the backed-up e-mail before going to the Gnosh—and to write that apology. From now on, she intended to do her e-mail before work and leave the laptop at home.

Morgan's whole body felt sluggish, but she dragged herself out of the bed. Stumbling to the desk where she'd set up her computer, she plugged into the Chandlers' phone line. No one would even know she was using it at this hour. She washed her face in cold water to wake up, then logged on.

Dreading what she knew she needed to do, Morgan started to compose her letter three different times, deleted it, then started again. Nothing sounded right. Tears welled up, and she brushed them away. Finally, she just decided to say what was on her heart:

Dear ANNA (and Marilyn, too, if you're reading!):
I don't know how to say this except to just say it. I am so sorry for interfering and giving bad advice. I didn't know the whole situation, and I had no business telling you to ignore your mom and not see a counselor. It sounds like you have a serious eating disorder that could be life threatening. Please listen to your mom and the counselor and get help.

Morgan paused, thinking again about that Higher Power stuff she'd read on the Internet and about Amber's Easter messages all week. She added:

I don't know what your beliefs are, ANNA, but maybe you could go to church on Easter and find help there. If you want to, keep me posted on how you're doing. I'll listen, but I won't give any more advice. Take care. –Morgan (jellybean).

Then she logged into GlobalBuddies.com, entering her alias and password. She wanted to check on last_wish, if he was there, and then she'd tackle the backlog of e-mail messages waiting for her. When the chat room opened, she was surprised to find about thirty names listed in the room. Did everyone get up this early? Then she realized that they were in a variety of time zones around the world.

Before she could scroll through the whole list of names, a tiny beep and blinking message icon popped up:

Last_wish has invited you to a private chat. Do you wish to join the room?

Morgan clicked on yes and a small screen opened where only her name and last_wish's appeared.

Morgan sighed. At least she was actually helping last_wish and his mom. Morgan bit her upper lip. She *had* planned to keep it all a surprise, but maybe she'd tell him about the money after all. She needed *someone* to be happy with her.

last_wish: U there?
jellybean14: yes. i'm staying this week @ a friend's house.

sorry I haven't written much. i've been so busy working. r
u feeling rested?

last__wish: had a better day than most. mom's @ work—i'm
just lonely, i guess

jellybean14: i've got a big surprise 4 U!

Morgan went on to tell him about the donation box and the
cards coming in from all over the country.

jellybean14: & i keep getting donations 4 UR mom!

last__wish: I can't believe it! U R the best friend we could
have! did u open bank account for mom?

jellybean14: nope—we've got a donations box @ the restaurant—and we got your cards sent there cause nobody @
my house 2 pick up mail.

last__wish: this is so cool. the last wish restaurant! People in
california—at least in our neighborhood—don't do stuff like
this. U have 2 work today?

jellybean14: yes, but just breakfast & lunch. we're closing
early all week. good thing 2. I need 2 work w/ friends
on a school project that's due Monday. Y R U up so early,
anyway? don't meds make u sleepy?

last__wish: yeah—but i woke up when mom left. i do think i
oughta go back 2 bed now tho. glad u were online—cured
my lonelies.

jellybean14: will write LTR. have 2 answer some e-mail and

get ready 4 work. write soon! i'll keep working on the $$.
last_wish: thanks! It will mean a lot 2 my mom. don't work
2 hard. have a good day.
jellybean14: U 2. bye

Morgan stretched and yawned, rubbing her neck. Her neck and back seemed to ache all the time these days, and her temples were already beginning to throb. She could hardly remember the last day she hadn't had a headache. But somehow it didn't matter so much now. Last_wish had sounded so excited by her news.

Stretching her neck from side to side, Morgan was vaguely aware of sounds of stirring elsewhere in the Chandler house.

For the next hour, Morgan replied to nearly twenty requests for more information about last_wish and his mom. She was touched by how many said they were sending cards, but with more than a dollar inside, sometimes as much as twenty. They wanted her to keep them informed about last_wish's condition, too. Some even suggested she set up a Web site.

"Morgan," Jamie called from the hallway, surprising her. "Bathroom's free."

"Be there in a minute." Morgan finished the last three e-mails just in time for three new ones to pop up. The subject lines showed they were also about donating money to last_wish. Clenching her teeth and ignoring her headache, she answered each one's questions. *This is for a very good cause,* she reminded herself when she wanted to quit.

"I'm leaving now," Jamie said, popping into the den. "Are you rea—" She stopped short. "You're not even dressed! The place opens in twenty minutes!"

"Oh, man, I got caught up—" Morgan looked longingly at Jamie. "Could you do me a favor? If I give you my key to open, can you go do that? I'm right behind you. I just have to get dressed," she said, logging off the computer and shutting its lid.

"Won't Benny be there getting the food started?" Jamie asked. "He can just let me in."

"You know Benny. He takes care of the food. Period. You could bang on the door all day and he wouldn't even look up."

"True. Give me your key then." Jamie nodded at the computer. "Was all that for last_wish?"

Morgan remembered the letter to ANNA's family, but answered, "Mostly."

Jamie stuck the key in her pocket. "I can open, but you'd better hurry. Amber's not that experienced, so she's still kinda slow."

Morgan jumped up, grabbed her clothes and shampoo, and headed for the shower down the hall. "I'll be there before you know it. Thanks a million."

But by the time Morgan dragged her weary body through the shower, got dressed, and walked to the Gnosh after finding her bike tire flat, it was nearly seven! She moaned inwardly when she glanced through the front window and saw the crowd filling all the booths and most of the tables. She hurried inside.

Jamie rushed by her, balancing three plates full of fried eggs and French toast. "It's about time!" she snapped, hurrying to set the plates down at booth number three. "I can't handle your booths plus half the tables! Hurry up!" After stacking dirty dishes in a plastic tub, she rushed back to the kitchen.

Amber was at the cash register, frowning as she tried to work the right buttons, and customers were lined up three-deep waiting on her. She glanced up and flashed a look of irritation at Morgan, but said nothing. Morgan grabbed some dirty glasses and ran to the kitchen for her apron and order pad. She halted when she saw the dishes piled high already in the sink. A small army must have stopped there for breakfast.

"We're out of water glasses and spoons already," Jamie said. "Can you wash some quick?"

"Sure." Morgan ran hot water in the sink. "Use the to-go cups and spoons while I run the dishwasher." She grabbed a double handful of spoons and dropped them into a dishwasher rack. "Or do you want me out front?"

"Load the dishes, then bus tables, then take orders." Jamie glanced at Benny, who stood hunched over the huge griddle, flipping pancakes and French toast. "And whatever you do, please don't get online."

"I didn't bring my laptop."

"Well, thank goodness for small favors."

For the next hour, Morgan ran at top speed to help get things caught up. Even when the crowd thinned, she didn't slow down.

She had to make up to Amber and Jamie for being late again. If her dad ever found out how neglectful she'd been at the Gnosh all week, she'd be in deep trouble.

At four o'clock Benny left, without a word, by way of the back door. About five, Morgan was still mopping when the phone rang. "Gnosh Pit." Morgan's voice was tired and flat.

"Well there she is . . . the hardest-working daughter a man could have. How's my little jellybean?"

"Hi, Dad." Morgan felt herself relax just hearing her dad's voice. "I haven't heard from you lately. I've missed you."

"Me, too. We all wanted to talk to you. We called Jamie's for a while, early this morning. The line was busy."

"Oh, that was my fault." Morgan thought quickly. "I was researching my seals project online since I didn't get to go with you to New York." As soon as the words were out, Morgan wanted to bite her tongue off. Now she was telling lies to her *father*. She'd never done that before.

"Well, watch that the Chandlers' line isn't tied up. You should probably work at the library for that. Honey, you sound exhausted. How're things going?"

"Pretty good. I'm just tired." She stretched and yawned loudly into the phone. "We were slammed and we're still cleaning up. I should probably go help." A minute later, they'd said their good-byes and she was off the phone. She overheard Jamie talking to Amber where they sat in a booth out front.

"I've worked a lot this week," Jamie was saying, "and so has Mom. We're going to have what she calls *bonding time* over dinner." She turned and saw Morgan in the doorway. "Will you be home for dinner tonight?"

"No, I'll grab something here because I want to stay and restock. You and your mom go ahead and bond away." Morgan smiled, knowing she would feel a little less guilty about the morning if she stayed late and worked hard.

"Well, OK then." Jamie slid out of the booth and stood close to the counter. "Hey, Morg. I'm sorry about being so crabby this morning. I was frustrated and breakfast wasn't going well . . . there's no excuse, though."

Morgan hung her head. "You don't need to apologize. I would have been mad at me, too." She glanced up, relieved. "Thanks, though. Sorry 'bout being late. I'll be at your house as soon as I'm finished."

"If we go anywhere, we'll leave the house unlocked. See you when you get done."

"I'll stay and help," Amber said, "then give you a lift home."

"You don't need to do that."

"I want to." She smiled tiredly as Jamie left. "There's not that much to do really, not if we split it."

Amber got the closing checklist from the kitchen and came back to the register. She read aloud from the list as she divided the chores. "OK, Morgan, you scour pans, load dishwasher, turn off the deep-fat fryer . . ." Morgan nodded, barely listening as she sorted through the money in the last_wish box. People had stuffed dollar bills in there along with their change!

". . . I'll sweep if you mop, then we can refill everything, and take out the garbage," Amber finished.

"I'll get busy right away," Morgan said, putting the donation money back in the box. What was it Amber had told her to do first? *Oh yeah, load the dishwasher.* Afterward, Morgan scoured the cooking pans, rinsed them, and sanitized them in the small countertop dishwasher. Weariness threatened to overcome her, but she pushed on. She glanced around the kitchen and noted the overflowing garbage cans. "Take out garbage," she muttered, grabbing the roll of black plastic bags with orange ties. When finished, she hoisted two of the heavy bags over her shoulders to carry out the back door.

Outside, she was surprised how dark it was already. She stopped a moment to study the stars. Holding her breath as she lifted the heavy metal lid of the Dumpster, Morgan then heaved the bags, one at a time, over the side. She let the lid fall with a *clang.*

She walked back up the short alley and opened the kitchen door, pausing a moment to study the night sky and find the Big Dipper. Then, suddenly, metal pans crashed to the floor from inside. Morgan's heart pounded at the sound of Amber's high-pitched wail.

chapter.10

Morgan tore into the kitchen at the sound of Amber's piercing scream. Across the room, Amber stood at the big triple sink, tears streaming down her face, with her left arm under the running water.

"What happened?" Morgan raced around the big sink to reach Amber. Her blonde hair hung down over her face. "What happened?" she asked again.

"I wasn't looking—I mean, I thought you emptied the hot grease, and I went ahead—" Amber drew in a hissing breath between her teeth. "Man this really hurts."

"Keep it under the cold water," Morgan said. "I'll get some ice, too. Dad says that's the best thing for burns."

Morgan grabbed a handful of ice cubes from the freezer—dropping half of them on the floor—and threw them into a clean dishtowel, then hurried back to her friend. Amber sucked in her breath sharply, and held out her arm. All the way from her wrist to her elbow, the skin on the back of her arm was rippled with small red blisters already rising along the surface. Morgan opened the towel and blanched as Amber closed her eyes, bit her lower lip, and lowered the back of her arm onto the ice.

"You have to believe me," Morgan stammered. "I didn't hear you tell me to dump the hot oil. I loaded dishes, and took out garbage—"

"It's OK," Amber answered, still biting her lip. "But I think I need to go home. I don't feel so good."

"Here. Sit down." Morgan kicked the stepstool toward them and gently wrapped the towel up and around Amber's arm. "Hold that and let me get the first aid kit." She pulled it down off the shelf, opened it, and read the names of the medications. "Here," she cried. "Burn Relief!" She snagged several packets of the medicine, four nonstick gauze pads, and the roll of adhesive tape. "You need to have that covered on the way home."

"You sure?"

"Yes. Dad drilled Maya and me on first aid and what to do in case of accidents. You need to cover it and keep out the air. Here, lemme get that ice off. Now hold your arm out." Morgan dumped the supplies in Amber's lap and tore the medicine open, pack by pack, dripping a thick coating across the whole burn area. Then she laid the gauze pads over the medication and loosely taped them to the bottom of Amber's arm.

"This will keep it clean and protected till you get home."
Remembering the redness and texture of the injury, Morgan
took a deep shuddering breath. "You might have to see a doctor.
Oh, Amber, I'm so sorry!" And she burst into tears.

Amber patted Morgan's shoulder with her good arm. "Don't
cry. I'll be fine. This medicine is totally helping. And I know
you'd never hurt me on purpose."

Morgan stared at the floor as Amber walked out the front door.
She honestly *hadn't* heard Amber's directions, but she knew it
was because she'd been busy counting the money in the donation
box. Without wanting to, Morgan instantly recalled ANNA's situation. Amber wasn't the only person she'd hurt lately.

Morgan locked up the Gnosh Pit and cut through the park
toward the Chandlers' house. Her loneliness pressed like a steel
vice-grip across her chest, and the guilt stewed sourly just below,
making her stomach hurt.

I'm so disgusted with myself! she thought. *I want my mom—
she'd know how to make me feel better. Or Dad. Anybody . . . just
to make this feeling go away.* The tears started flowing as she
imagined Amber's arm—seriously burned just because she was
spaced out thinking about last_wish. Even ANNA's life was in
jeopardy because of well-meant advice she'd given. She wiped off
her face as she turned into the Chandlers' driveway.

Morgan expected to find Jamie and her mom at home, but
the house was quiet. She remembered the bonding time when

she read a note on the kitchen table: "Morgan, Mom and I went to Mario's for dinner. Back soon!"

Morgan's shoulders sagged. She didn't want to be alone. This time last week, she would have been thrilled to have the empty house to herself to be online. But tonight it just made her want to cry again. Maybe she'd just go to bed early. She got halfway upstairs when she heard voices, so she returned to the kitchen.

"Hey! We brought lasagna," Jamie called.

Mrs. Chandler nodded toward the microwave. "Want me to warm some for you?"

"No thanks." Morgan plopped down at the table. "I've really made a mess of everything."

Jamie's mom sat next to her and looked concerned. "What's happened?"

"I accidentally hurt Amber."

"You did what?" Jamie sat opposite Morgan.

"I messed up while we were cleaning. I wasn't listening when Amber was reading my list of stuff to do, and I didn't empty the hot oil from the deep-fat fryer. She was putting pans away over the fryers, and when one fell from the shelf, she caught it mid-air, but not without dunking the back of her arm right down into the hot oil. She got burned pretty bad—the whole back of her arm. I didn't hear her instructions . . ." Morgan's voice trailed off. "I got distracted and was counting the donation money for last_wish."

At her mom's quizzical glance, Jamie explained, "It's an

online friend of hers that has cancer." She turned to Morgan. "Is Amber OK? Did she have to go to the doctor?"

"I'm not sure. It looked pretty bad, though."

"Let's call her later and see how she's doing." Janet Chandler's voice was very quiet. "Morgan, forgive me if I'm too personal here." She hesitated. "It just seems to me, from watching you this week, that you spend quite a lot of time on the computer."

Morgan stared at her lap.

"I'm sorry," Mrs. Chandler said. "It's really none of my business." She started to get up.

"No, it's OK." Morgan glanced up, embarrassed. "You're right. I don't really know why I do it. It's like I can't get enough of being online."

Jamie's mom nodded slowly. "This may sound like an odd question." She recrossed her legs. "Do you feel better after you've spent time online?"

Morgan picked at the hangnail on her thumb. "At first I did. I thought I was helping people. They were like friends." Morgan leaned on her elbow, her head resting on her clenched fist. In a voice so low that Jamie and her mother had to lean close to hear, she told them how her involvement in online chat rooms and bulletin boards had taken more and more of her time—and sleeping hours. She reminded Jamie about when they lost the meet—that she'd been so tired that her swim time was affected. Morgan told them everything, holding back the tears that wanted to erupt anew: Jared was mad at her for missing group meetings, Amber had been badly burned, ANNA's eating disorder could kill her, and even that her mom probably had missed her chance with the New York art gallery when that call didn't get through.

With her fingertip, she traced a swirl in the woodgrain on the kitchen table. "Jared even said I had an addiction, but I don't. I just need to cut back. I read about addictions for a friend once," she added, recalling the checklist questionnaire she'd found for ANNA, "and my problem isn't that serious. It's like I know what I need to do, but it's just so hard!"

Jamie's mom patted her hand. "Well, an addiction is *anything* that controls a person, and it's usually something used to relieve pain." She paused. "Often addictive behavior is an attempt to hide from reality—to put off dealing with issues that hurt."

Morgan glanced up quickly. Her parents and sister were gone. Her best friend was gone. Did Mrs. Chandler understand that her Internet friends eased her loneliness?

"Morgan, have you considered asking God to help you stop?"

"God?"

"Yes. Have you ever confided in Him? Because He can help."

Morgan looked down in embarrassment. "I don't know if that would work for me or not. I don't go to church much."

Jamie reached her hand across the table. "So come. Come with us to our church tomorrow night."

"That's a great idea," Mrs. Chandler agreed. "Would you like to go to Good Friday services?"

Morgan mulled it over. She knew Good Friday was supposed to be some big deal. So why not? It couldn't hurt. She felt so guilty over all the broken promises to her friends, as well as the lies that had become almost routine to hide the amount of time she was online. She hated herself for being so dishonest. It just wasn't *her*.

She looked up then. "Yes, I'd like to go."

They talked of lighter topics while eating reheated lasagna. After totally forgetting the TodaysGirls.com chat time, Jamie and Morgan decided to watch TV. Finally, at eleven Jamie stumbled off to bed. Morgan wished she felt sleepy, but she was wide awake. She was still worried sick about Amber. Twice she called Amber's phone number to check on her, but the line was busy both times.

Morgan tossed and turned on the couch, unable to drift off. She didn't like being alone in the eerie silence. She wondered if there would be any response from ANNA or her mom. After Janet Chandler went to bed, Morgan slipped into the den, turned on her laptop, and checked her e-mail. Nothing from ANNA or her mom, and oddly, nothing from last_wish either. Morgan hoped that didn't mean bad news, like a relapse or something. For two hours, she answered the fifteen e-mails that had come from many caring people. Each person—except one man who called her idea "computer fraud"—was sending money to the restaurant.

Morgan sat back, turned to look at the VCR, and winced. The

blue numbers glowed 2:30 A.M., and the knots at the base of her skull seemed to grow tighter as the clock changed to 2:31. She needed to lie down and get to sleep. Morning would be there in just four short hours as it was. But before she logged off, she recalled the conversation she'd had with Jamie's mom, then took a guess and typed in addictions.com just to see. Sure enough, the home page popped up with an icon for Internet Addiction Information.

Bracing herself, she clicked the button and read through the questions:

1) Do you use online services every day without any skipping?

2) Do you lose track of time after making a connection?

3) Have you been going out less and less?

4) Do you spend less and less time on meals at home or at work, or do you eat meals in front of the monitor?

5) Do you deny spending too much time on the Net?

6) Do others complain of your spending too much time online?

7) Do you check your mailbox several times a day?

8) Do you log on to the Net while you're already busy at work?

9) Do you sneak online when family members are not at home, feeling a sense of relief?

But it was the last question that stopped Morgan cold: *Do you continue to use the Internet excessively despite significant problems it may be causing in your real life?*

Stunned, Morgan clicked on the X to close the window. It was like someone had followed her around, taking notes on her life, and then put it into a questionnaire. And here she was, online at 3:00 A.M.; right after telling Jamie and her mom all the terrible things that had happened because she overused the Net. *Do you continue to use the Internet excessively despite significant problems it may be causing in your real life?* The question haunted Morgan long after the screen went black.

Not even two hours later, the alarm went off and Morgan dragged herself out of bed. She *couldn't* be late to the Gnosh again. She didn't even know if Amber would be able to come to work. When Morgan and Jamie got to work, Amber was already out front, waiting in her mom's parked car. Morgan stopped, ashamed at the sight of Mrs. Thomas.

Jamie took Morgan's arm. "Come on. Amber isn't going to bite you. She's probably not even mad—" Jamie cut off in mid-sentence. "Oh, man!" Morgan peered around Jamie as Amber emerged from the car. From elbow to wrist, her arm was wrapped in hospital-grade bandages.

chapter.11

Morgan looked out the Gnosh window on Saturday at the gray and gloom that had settled over Edgewood. Turning, she straightened the big stack of cards that had just come in for last_wish. From the weight of the red donation box, it was filling up. The breakfast crowd was past, and the lunch bunch hadn't begun to trickle in. It would be a perfect time to get online and let last_wish know how things were going.

Morgan had her laptop hidden in the office in her backpack, but she couldn't get to it without Amber or Jamie seeing her. Too bad they'd been online the night before when Maya had e-mailed Dad's unfair message. No time online *at all*? Morgan knew her friends had to see how unreasonable that was; yet, they'd expect her to go along with her dad's wishes. On the other hand . . . a month ago she would have expected herself to go along with it, too.

Jamie was spending every spare minute in the office, making the price changes on the menus for the spring and summer season. That made it nearly impossible to sneak in to log on to the Web. Money kept filling the donation box, and Morgan wondered if news of more donations was sitting in her e-mail. Or news from ANNA or last_wish.

When she spotted Jamie carrying a stack of printed menus into the kitchen, Morgan grabbed her chance. In the office, she set up her laptop on the floor behind the desk. She was just signing on when Jamie walked into the office for more quarters from the cash box.

"Morgan! I thought you were going to swear off this stuff."

"I know." Morgan flushed with embarrassment. "Please don't tell."

"That's not the point." Jamie squatted down beside Morgan. "Remember what you told my mom? You said you weren't happy when you did this. Not to mention what your dad said."

"I know, you're right." Morgan shut off the computer before answering a single e-mail. "I'll try harder."

"We'll talk later, but right now, we've got customers."

Most of the Saturday lunch crowd was high school students, and even though Amber couldn't carry plates of food, she handled taking orders and money with just a little trouble. Everyone asked about her bandages, and Morgan was grateful how Amber downplayed what had happened, leaving out Morgan's name altogether. Morgan could tell by the way that she held her arm; Amber's burn still hurt a lot. So, she and Jamie let Amber go home at two.

Morgan could hardly believe it when she glanced at the clock and it said 4:35. When the last two tables finally paid and left, she flipped the sign on the front door to CLOSED. "Hmm, look at those black clouds over the college." Morgan pointed toward the western sky, where black clouds banded across the horizon, obscuring the descending sun. "It's going to storm big time. We'd better get moving."

Together they carried the remaining dishes to the kitchen, and Jamie quickly stacked plates and glasses on the removable dishwasher racks. "Let's hurry and get these done because if we don't leave soon, we'll be dodging lightning all the way home." She set the greasy pans in the sudsy water to soak a minute. "What about the money in the register since Amber's gone?"

Morgan had already stuffed the bills into the zippered cash bag. "Dad left a voice mail here and said to leave it in the old roaster pan in the yellow cupboard. He'll come down tomorrow night when they get home and take it to the bank."

"I bet you'll be glad when they're home."

Morgan nodded. "I even miss Maya, although I'll probably need earplugs to stand her for a while. She'll be so New-York-City-fied that it could get deep!"

The pair scrubbed, scoured, swept, mopped, and stocked as the storm approached. They were hauling out two big black bags of trash when the first faraway lightning lit up the sky. "Still sounds far away," Morgan said as she hurried back inside with Jamie right behind her. "I know it's after seven," Morgan continued, heading toward the office, "but I'll just take one minute—no more—to let last_wish know how much money has come in so far, both in the cards and the donation box." Morgan saw Jamie's eyebrows lift. "I'll be fast. Just think what a neat Easter present this will be for him and his mom."

"OK, just this once, but you don't have time for chat rooms, too." Jamie followed Morgan into the Gnosh Pit office.

"I know." Morgan logged on, and Jamie watched over her shoulder as she checked her e-mail.

"Wow! You weren't kidding about this mail!" Jamie said, watching half a dozen new messages pop up.

"This is a slow day compared to most," Morgan said, hearing thunder in the distance. "We're really going to make a difference in last_wish's life."

"Well, drop him a quick note, and I'll go hide the money in the roaster and empty the dishwasher."

"Thanks, Jamie." But instead of writing an e-mail message, Morgan clicked her shortcut over to GlobalBuddies.com. Sure enough, last_wish was there. She quickly sent a private instant message.

jellybean14: Happy day B4 Easter!
last__wish: hi! haven't talked 2 you in a while.

jellybean14: have U been sicker?

last__wish: some, but I'm better today. it's harder on mom than on me. but she took me 2 the beach 2 day. ever seen the CA beaches?

jellybean14: only in movies. "sigh" maybe sum good news will help UR mom & U!

last__wish: what good news?

jellybean14: I have nearly 200 cards already, and over half of them have more than $1 in them

last__wish: U R kidding!

jellybean14: it's 4 real! can't stay long. storm's coming. I stashed the cash so I can head home

last__wish: U mean donations?

jellybean14: no, it's restaurant $$ from today. I had 2 hide it. Dad's not home yet.

last__wish: UR family coming home soon?

jellybean14: tomorrow finally!

last__wish: bet UR glad. wish U were here. mom's taking me 4 a drive up in the mountains tomorrow.

jellybean14: mountains AND beaches! No fair!

Just then, a loud pounding on the Gnosh's front door made Morgan jump. What in the world—?

She heard Jamie unlock the door and voices she couldn't make out talked quickly. Then Jamie called down the hall. "Morgan! Come on. There's lots of lightning and it's starting to rain. Mom drove down to pick us up when she couldn't get through on the phone."

Oh, no, not again! And it had to be Jamie's mother who was try-ing to get through!

jellybean14: bye 4 now!

She logged off fast, reconnected the phone, and jumped when sharp flashes of lightning lit up the office right through the blinds. Thunder boomed like cannons immediately after-ward. "That was close!" Morgan muttered. Then the office lights blinked once, twice—and went out.

Morgan stumbled out of the dark office and groped her way down the hall. The front of the restaurant was pitch dark too, as well as the street outside. When the next bolt of lightning flashed, she spotted Jamie and her mom outlined by the front door.

"Come on. We can beat the downpour if we go now."

"Thanks for coming to get us." Morgan skirted the tables and chairs as she hurried to the front. "Let's get home!"

It wasn't until they were at Jamie's house and using flashlights to find their way through the garage that Morgan realized she'd left her computer behind at the Gnosh.

The power was only out an hour, and by then Jamie's little sis-ters had returned home from a trip with their friends. They popped popcorn and the two little girls laid their sleeping bags side by side on the living room floor to watch a movie. Two hours later, when the final credits rolled, Mrs. Chandler carefully stepped over her sleeping daughters. "I'm going to bed. You kids should too, since we have church tomorrow."

"No argument tonight, Mom." Jamie took her hair out of its ponytail. "I'm beat."

"Me, too," Morgan said, grabbing her own sleeping bag from behind the couch and spreading it across the sofa.

However, Morgan turned out the den lights and lay on top of her sleeping bag, fully dressed, for half an hour. She couldn't explain it, even to herself, but she felt so lonely and cut off from everyone that it was hard not to cry. Everyone in the house was probably asleep by now, and no one in her family would be home until the next night. The only people she knew would be awake were her GlobalBuddies. They usually needed a friend to talk to, too. She just didn't think she could sleep until she checked in one more time. Her decision made, she crept down the hall to Jamie's room and shook her friend hard. "Jamie, wake up. We have to go back to the Gnosh."

"Wh—What?" Jamie struggled up on one elbow. "Go where?"

"To the Gnosh. I need my laptop. We aren't open tomorrow, and all my notes for my group project are in the computer. I only have tomorrow to do my whole report."

"It's too late to go now. I'll tell Mom to stop by in the morning on the way to church. Go back to bed." And she rolled over.

Morgan stood, undecided, in the darkness of Jamie's bedroom.

Should she just sneak out and get it herself? She could be back in half an hour. It sounded like the rain had stopped a while ago. She could take the flashlight that was still in the den. No one would notice. She fingered the key in her pocket. She'd just run down to the Gnosh and use her key to get in—

Morgan froze. Something buzzed around her mind. Oh no! *I didn't use my key to lock up before leaving the Gnosh!*

In all the confusion with the power outage, she'd totally forgotten to lock the front door as they'd dashed to Mrs. Chandler's car to beat the storm.

"Jamie! Wake up! I need your help."

"Man, I was just starting to have the best dream. I hate that." Jamie rolled over and Morgan pulled off the covers, quickly explaining about leaving the front door unlocked. "We'll be there and back before anyone can miss us. Please? I'll be so in trouble if I leave it unlocked all night. It could have been robbed already! Come on! I don't want to walk by myself at this hour."

"This stinks," Jamie muttered. "You owe me big." She grabbed a pair of jeans and her baseball cap. "Be quiet on the way out, and don't wake up Mom or the girls."

Although it was barely drizzling when they left, halfway to the Gnosh, the clouds burst open again. The girls ran the rest of the way, drenched by sheets of rain. Once at the front door, Morgan twisted the knob and pushed—but the door wouldn't budge.

"Hurry up," Jamie said. "I'm like totally soaked already."

"Hold on." Feeling sheepish, Morgan fished out her key and unlocked the door.

"I thought you said you didn't lock it!"

A single icy shiver ran up Morgan's spine. "I didn't. I know I didn't."

"Then how—?"

Morgan opened the door. Just as she reached for the main light switch, a black shadow rose up not ten feet away. "Don't touch those lights," a voice snarled. "Not if you know what's good for you."

Morgan halted and Jamie plowed into her.

"Move behind the counter. *Now!*" the voice snapped. "Sit on the floor. I've got a gun."

Jamie gasped and gripped Morgan's hand. "Don't hurt us. We'll just leave."

"I said *sit on the floor!*"

Suddenly Morgan swung in the direction of the voice. Beneath the pounding of her heart, something else had registered. She had the uncanny sensation that she'd heard that voice somewhere before. But where?

Then she knew.

Whipping around, she flipped on the overhead lights. "What are you doing here, Tyler?" Morgan's voice shook with fear and anger. "Talk fast. This had better be good, or I'm calling 911."

"Morgan!" Jamie cried. "What are you doing?"

"Meet Tyler, one-third of my biology group for the Save the

Seals project." For the first time, Morgan saw what was on the table, too. "Hey! Give me that money! You can't have that!"

Ty snorted. "Why? It's for some cancer victim? Get real."

"It *is* for a cancer victim, not that you'd care. Now give it back."

"Finders keepers, stupid." Ty pushed her away. Chuckling to himself, he stuffed handfuls of bills from the donation box into his jacket pockets. "This will spend nicely on those California beaches, or maybe up in the mountains while my dear mama takes me for a ride."

Morgan's mouth fell open. What had he just said? California beaches? Rides in the mountains? Morgan felt sick as the pieces fell heavily into place. "*You're* last_wish," she finally said, the breath going out of her like a punctured balloon.

"Bingo! We have a winner."

Jamie came around in front of the counter, looking from Ty to Morgan and back to Ty. "*This* is last_wish?" she asked, horror mixed with unbelief.

Morgan stared at the wad of bills in Ty's hand. "I can't believe it. I just can't believe it." Nothing—*absolutely nothing*—she'd tried to do to help anyone had turned out right.

Ty moved to step around Morgan. Morgan considered tackling him, then thought better of it. He was six inches taller and probably twice her weight. She didn't stand a chance.

"Say, didn't you mention some restaurant money hidden here, too? Let's go find it."

Jamie wore a stunned expression. "You told this guy we had money hidden here?"

"No, I didn't tell *this* guy!" Morgan stung at the accusation. "I told some kid in *California* dying from *cancer*." Morgan looked with disgust at the gangly boy. "What's the matter with you?" she demanded.

"I need this money every bit as much as old last_wish does." His voice was suddenly bitter. "Even in Edgewood there are families without dads who need cash."

"That's no excuse to steal." Morgan's eyes narrowed. "Say, did *you* take that money I couldn't find, the money for the Adopt-A-Seal program?"

Ty laughed aloud. "Oh, you noticed? Careless of you to stick it in your book that way."

Morgan pointed an accusing finger at him. "You were in here with Jared the day our tip money disappeared, too!"

"You should pay better attention. You have no security! Heck, you people don't even lock the front door!" Ty laughed outright then. "I just walked in and turned the bolt from the inside. So, you can't even get me for breaking and entering. Or stealing either, since I'm last_wish and these cards even have my name on them!"

Morgan gasped. He couldn't get away with this, could he? "I can't believe you fooled me. I really believed you."

"That's the trick of the Internet, *Jellybean*. You can only know what the other person chooses to tell you."

"Well you're trespassing, Ty, and you impersonated some dying kid, which I'm sure is against the law. You won't get away with this." Morgan stepped closer to the phone.

At that, Ty stopped short. For the first time, doubt flickered over his face. "You're really calling 911?"

"Well, not if you hand over the money and leave. Now."

"What about you?" he demanded, turning to Jamie. She stood silent with her eyes closed. "Hey! Wake up! I'm talking to you!"

Jamie jumped. "I—I'm praying."

Ty sniffed. "Like you really believe that God stuff, like He really listens to you?"

Jamie nodded. "I know He listens. And if you prayed, He'd listen to you, too. Jesus loves all of us, Tyler."

Right then Morgan wished with all her heart that *she* could pray. What a mess she'd made of everything! But would God really listen to her? She bet God wouldn't hear a liar who had put so many people in so many different types of danger. She knew they were incredibly lucky that their "burglar" was just a dork and not a real gun-carrying criminal.

Ty snorted and threw the donation money and cards back down on the table. "I'm outta here. I didn't come for any Jesus revival." With that, he slammed out the front door. Morgan jumped up, and with shaking hands, twisted the deadbolt. With knees wobbling so they'd barely support her, Morgan slid down the front of the counter to the floor next to Jamie. They sat in stunned silence.

"Oh, Jamie, I don't know what to say." Morgan shuddered. "I'm so sorry about putting you in danger. He could have been a real burglar!"

"Hey, it's over now. God was protecting us. Ty did give us a good scare, though." Jamie turned and looked at her friend. "I hope you see *now* the Internet's power over you lately. It's made you blind to things."

Morgan nodded slowly. The mountain of evidence—the harm she'd done to her friends especially—made it impossible to deny. "I keep trying to do better because I *want* to do better. I try to control the time I spend online, but I can't seem to keep my promises, even to myself."

"In other words, you really don't have power over the sin in your life?"

Morgan leaned her head to one side. "I didn't think of it like that, but no, I sure don't."

"Well, remember what our pastor said last night?" Jamie asked. "He said accepting Jesus as your Savior would give you that power."

"You mean what he called being 'born again'? Then I'd have power to control this addiction, or whatever it is?" Morgan wanted desperately to believe that, but how could she? Besides, sometimes she was so lonely that being online was the only thing that helped her feel better.

"Jesus wants to give you more than that," Jamie said. "More than just power to control this thing, even though that's very important. He wants to heal the hurt inside you. Remember what you told me and Mom about Thursday night—that makes you do kinda crazy things just to be online?" Jamie's voice softened.

"Jesus wants to be your best Friend, always with you. Then you'll find that empty hole getting smaller and smaller till you won't need to constantly be online anymore. He can fill that place inside you, Morgan. He's the only One who can."

Morgan's throat felt so tight she couldn't swallow. Jamie didn't talk about her faith very often, but Morgan knew that, like Amber, Jamie believed and prayed. And right then Morgan would give anything to be like that.

Raindrops fell gently against the window, adding their rhythm to Jamie's words as she continued, "Last night Mr. Holsey said that Jesus bridges the gap between God and us. He came here so that we could have God's forgiveness for our sins. He died to give us new life in Him. And we're all just the same, Morgan.

"Back when Dad walked out on us, I wanted to die. How could he do that? You didn't know me then, but my life was a real mess. I did some stuff—wrong stuff—to get people's attention, but accepting Christ into my heart has given me a real peace and finally healed that loneliness. He'll do that for you, too," she added quietly. "No matter what you've done, Jesus takes us as we are and meets us where we're at. If you want to, you can talk to Him."

Morgan swallowed hard, aching for the peace that Jamie described. Morgan glanced up at Jamie. Her eyes were shut.

Then, sitting right there on the floor of the restaurant, Morgan made her decision. She closed her eyes and prayed silently. "God, I'm so sorry for all the problems I've caused. Thank You for sending Your Son to die for me. I want You living in my heart. I want to give my life to You and start over again. Thank You. Amen."

She opened her eyes and waited, trying to make out how she felt. She hadn't sprouted wings or anything, but a feeling of peace had settled inside her. "I did it," she said to Jamie.

Jamie hugged her friend. "Just remember, Jesus will be your best Friend, your Comforter, and the best listener. From now on, you'll never be alone."

"That sounds so good." Morgan smiled, stretched, and stood up. The rain had quit, and street lamps at the corner spilled their light across the wet pavement. She scooped up the cards and donation money. "How about if we donate this to a *real* terminally ill child, like at the hospital here in town?"

"Great idea." Jamie's mouth opened in a wide yawn, then she grinned and shook her head. "I don't know about you, but I need my beauty sleep. Ready?"

Morgan thought for a brief second about running to the office for her laptop. But only for a brief second. It could wait till the next day when they stopped after church. She turned to her friend. "I'm ready. Let's go."

epilogue

Hey, Morgan! Chat time!" Maya called from her bedroom. "Get on in the kitchen!"

Morgan got a Coke from the refrigerator, shuddering at the tofu and bean sprouts rotting in there. *Ugh.* She moved her microwave popcorn and crunchy M&M's next to where her laptop was plugged into the family phone line. Even though she was grounded from being on the Internet, her mom had made an exception with the TodaysGirls.com nightly chat. Afterward she had to get right off. She logged on to see chat already scrolling down.

jellybean: hello girlz!
TX2step: itz about time
rembrandt: i was just finishing the story, M. anyway, my

mom realized we weren't home & freaked out. she called coach & said we were missing. he came barging in @ the Gnosh.

faithful1: so what's up w/ ty?

jellybean: we didn't call the police because he didn't break & enter. it was unlocked.

rembrandt: but he was trespassing

jellybean: coach called the principal. i don't know what will happen 2 him.

TX2step: so how much trouble are U guys in?

rembrandt: i'm grounded 4 sneaking out & scaring mom 2 death, but just for a couple days.

jellybean: i'm major grounded

nycbutterfly: swim practice will B M's social life 4 a while. i leave 4 a week and look @ all that happens!

TX2step: U ought 2 leave more often

nycbutterfly: just wait till i go 2 school. THEN U'll miss me

TX2step: believe it or not, i missed all U guyz last week. good 2 B back.

faithful1: hope UR still glad tomorrow. coach called an early morning practice. wait till Bren hears. she flies in after midnight.

TX2step: ACK!

nycbutterfly: just hope lil sis gets her time back up.

jellybean: no prob. i'm staying off the Net & going 2 bed early!

Before Morgan knew it, the clock in the corner of her monitor showed that a half-hour had passed. She typed "Happy Easter, girls" and logged off, then leaned back against the wall. She grabbed another handful of popcorn, letting it dribble through her fingers back into the bowl. As she looked around the kitchen, Morgan felt the peace and joy she'd felt that morning at the sunrise Easter service slowly evaporate. Had it been real? Was Jesus *truly* living in her heart? Suddenly, Morgan felt no different than before her midnight encounter in the restaurant.

She was still alone.

Alex was obviously back in town, but she hadn't called when she got home. Morgan would have gladly met her bus. Jacob wasn't due back till almost midnight, and her parents were still gone, too. Her dad was checking the restaurant and depositing all that money. Her mom had finally called and connected with the gallery owner, but never got to meet him. However, he'd finally agreed to look at her art if she sent him copies on disk. Morgan's mom was out getting it scanned right then. Oh well, at least they weren't moving to New York, Morgan thought. She'd been so relieved to learn that she'd misunderstood their conversation. Maya was home, though. Maybe she'd want to do something with her.

Halfway up the stairs, however, Morgan could hear her big sister on the phone. Morgan leaned her head to one side and listened. *Must be Darryl,* she decided, relieved that he'd accepted her apology when she'd called him after dinner. Morgan retraced her steps to the kitchen, peered into the refrigerator again, then turned and eyed her computer.

Her parents wouldn't be home for at least an hour, Morgan would be on the phone that long, and Jacob would be even later. She could use the family line and click into GlobalBuddies.com without anyone knowing. She didn't want her online friends to think she'd abandoned them. Being abandoned felt rotten, and she didn't want anyone feeling that way because of her.

Still, Morgan knew she was grounded and she'd agreed to abide by her parents' rules. If only she didn't feel so lonely . . .

As she sat in the dark kitchen, lit only by the tiny light over the stove, Jamie's words from the night before slowly came back to her. Jesus wanted to be her Friend, Jamie had said. He would meet Morgan where she was.

"Well, where I'm *at* is lonely," Morgan whispered. "Lord, please help me. If You're really living inside me, please be my Friend now."

Closing her eyes, Morgan breathed deeply and waited. Slowly the squeezing sensation in her chest eased, and the tears that had been welling up in her eyes dried. A warm layer of peace settled down over her like a flannel blanket.

Smiling slowly, Morgan whispered, "Thank You." Then she unhooked her laptop from the phone jack and carried it into the den with her. In no time, she found herself engrossed in rewriting her Save the Seals report. She ended it with an appeal for the class to join them in adopting a seal and donating money to apply toward their medical needs. She was just finishing when she heard a knock on the back door.

After typing her last few words, Morgan ran to the kitchen. After peeking through the curtain, she flipped on the porch light, spotted Alex, and grinned. She threw open the door.

"Got time for a friend?" Alex asked. "Or are you grounded from having company, too?"

"Nope! Real live friends are still allowed." She stepped back as Alex came inside, then gave her a quick hug. "Boy, do you look tan! You'll have to tell me everything. I missed you!"

But before Alex could open her mouth, there was another knock. "What is this, Grand Central Station?" Alex asked.

Morgan shrugged and opened the door again. On the back step was a huge poster with feet and legs protruding below. "Is this the Save the Seals Headquarters?" came a muffled voice from behind the poster.

Morgan laughed, turned the poster around, and whistled. "This is great, Jared!" she said. "I just finished my report, and it'll be perfect with this."

Jared shut the door behind him and smiled. "I aim to please." His grin faded. "I have Tyler's notes and the overhead he made, but he won't be in school tomorrow. He's really embarrassed about the whole thing."

"He should be! I still can't believe he was last_wish."

Just then the headlights of her dad's classic '55 Chevy swept into the driveway. Maya's familiar footsteps came skipping down the stairs, and from the sound of her singing, the phone call from Darryl had been a success. Maya waltzed into the kitchen at the same moment her parents opened the kitchen door.

Morgan gazed from her friends to her family, suddenly overwhelmed by her good fortune to have so much love surrounding her. The people she met online were friendly and interesting, but these people were *real*. Now she knew that, even when none of them were around, she always had the very best Friend a person could have, a Friend that would never leave her.

"Looks like it's time for a welcome home party," Morgan said, throwing open the refrigerator door. "Tofu and sprouts, anyone?"

Net Ready, Set, Go!

I hope my words and thoughts please you.
Psalm 19:14

The characters of TodaysGirls.com chat online in the safest—and maybe most fun—of all chat rooms! They've created their own private Web site and room! Many Christian teen sites allow you to create your own private chat rooms, and there are other safe options.

Work with your parents to develop a list of safe, appropriate chat rooms. Earn Internet freedom by showing them you can make the right choices. *Honor your father and your mother (Deuteronomy 5:16).*

Before entering a chat room, you'll select a user name. Although you can use your real name, a nickname is safer. Most people choose one that says something about who they are, like Amber's name, faithful1. Don't be discouraged if the name you select is already taken. You can use a similar one by adding a number at its end.

No one will notice your grammar in a chat room. Don't worry if you spell something wrong or forget to capitalize. Some people even misspell words on purpose. You might see a sentence like How R U?

But sometimes it's important to be accurate. Web site and e-mail addresses must be exact. Pay close attention to whether letters are upper- or lowercase. Remember that Web site addresses don't use some punctuation marks, such as hyphens and apostrophes. (That's why the "Today's" in TodaysGirls.com has no apostrophe!) And instead of spaces between words, underlines are used to_make_a_space. And sometimes words just run together like onebigword.

When you're in a chat room, remember that real people are typing the words that appear on your screen. Treat them with the same respect you expect from them. Don't say anything you wouldn't want repeated in Sunday school. *Do for other people what you want them to do for you (Luke 6:31).*

Sometimes people say mean, hurtful things—things that make us angry. This can happen in chat rooms, too. In some chat rooms, you can highlight a rude person's name and click a button that says, "ignore," which will make his or her comments disappear from your screen. You always have the option to switch rooms or sign off. If a particular person becomes a continual problem, or if someone says something especially vicious, you should report this problem user to the chat service. *Ask God to bless those who say bad things to you. Pray for those who are cruel (Luke 6:28–29).*

Remember that Internet information is not always factual. Whether you're chatting or surfing Web sites, be skeptical about information and people. Not everything on the Internet is true. You don't have to be afraid of the Internet, but you should always be cautious. Practice caution with others even in Christian chat rooms.

It's okay to chat about your likes and dislikes, but *never* give out personal information. Do not tell anyone your name, phone number, address, or even the name of your school, team, church, or neighborhood. Be cautious. . . . *You will be like sheep among wolves. So be as smart as snakes. But also be like doves and do nothing wrong. Be careful of people (Matthew 10:16–17).*

STRANGER ONLINE

16/junior
e-name: faithful1
best friend: Maya
site area: Thought for the Day

Confident. Caring. Swimmer. Single-handedly built TodaysGirls.com Web site. Loves her folks. Big brother Ryan drives her nuts! Great friend. Got a problem? Go to Amber.

AMBER THOMAS

JAMIE CHANDLER

PORTRAIT OF LIES

15/sophomore
e-name: rembrandt
best friend: Bren
site area: Artist's Corner

Quiet. Talented artist. Works at the Gnosh Pit after school. Dad left when she was little. Helps her mom with younger sisters Jordan and Jessica. Baby-sits for Coach Short's kids.

ALEX DIAZ

TANGLED WEB

14/freshman
e-name: TX2step
best friend: Morgan
site area: to be determined . . .

Spicy. Hot-tempered Texan. Lives with grandparents because of parents' problems. Won state in freestyle swimming at her old school. Snoops. Into everything. Breaks the rules.

R U 4 REAL?

16/junior

e-name: nycbutterfly

best friend: Amber

site area: What's Hot—What's Not
(under construction)

MAYA CROSS

Fashion freak. Health nut. Grew up in New York City. Small town drives her crazy. Loves to dance. Dad owns the Gnosh Pit. Little sis Morgan is also a TodaysGirl.

BREN MICKLER

LUV@FIRST SITE

15/sophomore

e-name: chicChick

best friend: Jamie

site area: Smashin' Fashion (under construction)

Funny. Popular. Outgoing. Spaz. Cheerleader. Always late. Only child. Wealthy family. Bren is chatting—about anything, online and off, except when she's eating junk food.

CHAT FREAK

14/freshman

e-name: jellybean

best friend: Alex

site area: Feeling All Write

MORGAN
CROSS

The Web-ster. Spends too much time online. Overalls. M&Ms. Swim team. Tries to save the world. Close to her family—when her big sister isn't bossing her around.

Cyber Glossary

Bounced mail An e-mail that has been returned to its sender.

Chat A live conversation—typed or spoken through microphones—among individuals in a chat room.

Chat room A "place" on the Internet where individuals meet to "talk" with one another.

Crack To break a security code.

Download To receive information from a more powerful computer.

E-mail Electronic mail which is sent through the Internet.

E-mail address An Internet address where e-mail is received.

File Any document or image stored on a computer.

Floppy Disk A small, thin plastic object which stores information to be accessed by a computer.

Hacker Someone who tries to gain unauthorized access to another computer or network of computers.

Header Text at the beginning of an e-mail which identifies the sender, subject matter, and the time at which it was sent.

Homepage A Web site's first page.

Internet A worldwide electronic network that connects computers to each other.

Link Highlighted text or a graphic element which may be clicked with the mouse in order to "surf" to another Web site or page.

Log on/Log in To connect to a computer network.

Modem A device which enables computers to exchange information.

The Net The Internet.

Newbie A person who is learning or participating in something new.

Online To have Internet access. Can also mean to use the Internet.

Surf To move from page to page through links on the Web.

The Web The World Wide Web or WWW.

Upload To send information to a more powerful computer.